Friends
No Matter What

Mark Littleton

HARVEST HOUSE PUBLISHERS
Eugene, Oregon 97402

FRIENDS NO MATTER WHAT

Copyright© 1995 by Mark Littleton
Published by Harvest House Publishers
Eugene, Oregon 97402

Library of Congress Cataloging-in-Publication Data

Littleton, Mark R., 1950-
    Friends no matter what / Mark Littleton.
        p.   cm. — (Crista chronicle ; 6th)
    Summary: Crista befriends Kayzee, a new black student, whose
presence at Lake Wallenpaupack Elementary School disturbs some
prejudiced members of the community.
    ISBN 1-56507-256-1
    [1. Prejudices—Fiction. 2. Race relations—Fiction. 3. Afro-
Americans—Fiction. 4. Friendship—Fiction.]   I. Title. II. Series:
Littleton, Mark R., 1950-   Crista chronicles series ; bk. 6.
PZ7.L7364Fr   1994   94-5306
[Fic]—dc20   CIP
                                                                   AC

Printed in the United States of America.

95 96 97 98 99 00 — 10 9 8 7 6 5 4 3 2 1

Contents

·1·

The Race

Through the window in the wall next to the classroom door, Crista Mayfield could see the principal, Mr. Burleson, knocking. A girl stood next to him. She was African-American, with two long braids down either side of her face.

Crista glanced at Jeff Pallaci, sitting across the aisle from her. Jeff looked back and winked.

"New student?" he whispered.

Mrs. Roberts walked across the front of the classroom as Mr. Burleson stepped inside. He spoke softly to Mrs. Roberts, introduced her to the new girl, and nodded his head several times as they talked quietly. Then he turned and left.

The brown-haired prim teacher took the girl's hand and led her to the front of the classroom.

"This is a new classmate of yours, children," she announced with a smile. "Her name is Kayzee Jackson. Her mother is the new nurse here, replacing Mrs. Tolman. Please welcome her."

All the children responded in semi-friendly voices, "Welcome, Kayzee."

Mrs. Roberts stood back. "Would you like to tell us a little about yourself, Kayzee?" she asked.

Kayzee smiled shyly. "I'm from Atlanta in Georgia. My mother is a nurse. My father is in the Navy. He works on nuclear submarines. He's gone right now for six months. We came here because..."

She paused and looked around.

"Because..."

Mrs. Roberts smiled again. "Yes?"

"Because my brother was getting in with bad people."

"What's your brother's name?"

"I have two. Jamal and Lukie. Jamal is sixteen. He's the one who was getting in with some bad people. And Lukie's in second grade here, too."

"Do you have a hobby?" Mrs. Roberts asked.

"I collect butterflies," Kayzee answered.

Crista looked at Jeff and smiled. Jeff also collected butterflies. The Lake Wallenpaupack area in Pennsylvania where they lived was especially good for collecting. Jeff had over twenty different kinds of butterflies hanging in plain picture frames in his room.

"And I play soccer," Kayzee finished.

"We have a boy's soccer team," Mrs. Roberts said. "But none for girls."

"Oh." Kayzee hung her head a little. Then she looked up. "I also play softball."

"Oh, the kids play that all the time, don't you, children?" Mrs. Roberts said, looking over her glasses at the class.

"Yes, Mrs. Roberts," several answered back in chorus. Crista smiled and she saw Jeff chuckling, too.

"Well, then," Mrs. Roberts said, "I believe I'll put you back here behind Danny Kluziewski, next to Crista Mayfield. Danny, would you stand?"

Danny stood and turned to the empty desk behind him. As Kayzee slowly walked back to her desk, Mrs. Roberts told her that she'd get all her books and supplies at recess.

"Take your math workbooks out, class," Mrs. Roberts said, walking to the storage cabinet behind her desk. She took out an extra copy of the workbook and walked it back to Kayzee. "We're on page two-twenty-six. Now, Jeff, would you care to come to the board and perform the first problem."

"I really wouldn't care to," Jeff said under his breath. Crista grinned, but no one else heard him. He ambled forward and, book in hand, started to write out the problem.

Two hours later, after math, English, social studies, and passing out some papers for parents to fill out about a field trip, Crista and the rest of the class hurried outside for recess. Crista had never known a black kid before. In fact, in the area, there were very few black people and none in the sixth grade. Kayzee and her brother Lukie, Crista thought, were the first black kids in the whole school.

Mr. Rader, the gym teacher, was organizing running races during recess that day. As the girls lined up for a fifty-yard dash, Kayzee held back a little. Crista walked over to her.

"Come on," she encouraged. "Don't you like to run?"

Kayzee's eyes lit up. "Sure."

"Are you any good?"

"Not as good as my brother, Jamal."

"But he's older." Crista smiled as Kayzee followed her over to the line.

Mr. Rader looked them over. "Back behind the line, Julie," he said to one of the fastest girls in the class, Julie Linkower. Crista usually managed to come in third or fourth, but she had never beaten Julie.

Mr. Rader shouted, "Ready...get set..." *Tweet!* His whistle blew.

The girls took off. Crista sensed Kayzee next to her, pumping easily. Crista was running hard. She stared at the finish line ahead. As always, Julie was in the lead. But in the last twenty yards, Kayzee came up fast. She was short, but her legs were thin and fast. As they hit the line, Mr. Rader ran up.

"Okay, you win!" he shouted to Kayzee. "What's your name?"

"Kayzee Jackson."

"Hey, you are fast," Mr. Rader said.

Crista noticed Julie standing off to the left, talking to her friends. Mr. Rader returned to the starting line and shouted, "Now boys line up for your race. Then we'll run the best two boys against the best two girls."

Danny Kluziewski and another boy named Kent Carney took first and second. Finally it was time to pit the girls against the boys.

Kayzee, Julie, Danny, and Kent lined up. Mr. Rader blew his whistle. The four took off. Danny was in the lead at first, but as he neared the finish line, Kayzee blew by him. When it was over, she had won. Danny Kluziewski had been the champion of running since third grade.

Kayzee stopped at the end, panting. Julie walked over. She had been third.

"You are really fast," Julie said.

Kayzee nodded, still panting.

Crista ran up. "That was great!"

Danny stood off to the edge, scowling and grumbling to some of the other boys about being tricked. Jeff ambled over to Crista and Kayzee.

"Glad you beat Danny," Jeff said, patting Kayzee on the back. "He needed to be beaten."

Mr. Rader gathered everyone together. "Looks like we have a new fifty-yard champion," he said. "Kayzee Jackson. Let's do a little cheer. One-two-three, rah, rah, Kayzee. Okay, let's do it."

Everyone cried, "One-two-three, rah, rah, Kayzee!"

As the cheer finished, the bell rang and recess was over. The kids filed into the school.

Jeff caught up to Crista as she walked inside the classroom with another of her friends, Ruth Anne Depew. Jeff said, "Danny's pretty mad. He says

Kayzee tricked him."

"How?" Crista asked. "I didn't see any trick. Just because a girl..."

"I'm just telling you, that's all," Jeff said. "I think it's great. He needed to be put in his place. Always bragging about being number one."

Crista walked to her desk, thinking. As she sat down, she heard Danny say to one of his friends, "This isn't the end of it."

She wondered what that was supposed to mean. After all, it was only a race, wasn't it? It wasn't the end of the world.

·2·
Danger on the Road

After school, Crista and Jeff went out into the parking lot to catch their bus. Kids were lining up, getting ready to board. Crista noticed Kayzee standing in the back—alone. Crista walked over, tugging Jeff along behind her.

"Kayzee," she said. "Would you like to sit with us? We're going on the same bus, it looks like."

"Sure," Kayzee said, looking up and smiling. "I feel kind of out of place here."

"Really. Everyone's pretty friendly," Crista said. "If you give them a chance."

"I didn't mean that," Kayzee replied. She looked down at the ground and wouldn't meet Crista's eyes.

Crista didn't say anything more till they were seated on the bus. "How come you feel out of place?" she asked Kayzee, who had taken the seat beside her. Jeff was sitting behind them. "Not like Atlanta, huh?"

"That's for sure."

Suddenly, Crista realized what Kayzee meant.

She was the only African-American in the whole class. She wondered what she should say. Then Kayzee herself spoke up.

"Not many black people up this way, I guess."

Crista shook her head, slightly embarrassed. "I guess not many come up to this area. Jobs are tough, my dad says."

"What does your dad do?" Kayzee asked.

"He's a doctor. He delivers babies and helps pregnant mothers and stuff like that."

"My dad's in the Navy."

"I know," Crista said. "You said..."

"Right."

Jeff leaned into the space in between the girls' heads. "Hey, what does your father do in the Navy?"

"He's a lieutenant commander."

"Wow," Jeff said. "That sounds important."

"He helps the captain or something. I haven't quite figured it out."

Jeff and Crista laughed.

"Where do you live on the lake?" Crista asked as they passed the Wallenpaupack dam at one end of the lake.

"Midway Drive, I think." Kayzee frowned. "I already forget the number."

"That's one road down from us!" Crista exclaimed. "Jeff and I live on Rock Road."

"I don't know where that is," Kayzee said. She set her hands in her lap and watched as the bus roared up a long hill.

Crista noticed her thick, black braids. They were pretty and neatly woven. Kayzee had creamy, brown skin, flawless. She was cute, Crista thought.

Kids talked and shrieked and yelled on the bus as Crista and Kayzee and Jeff conversed quietly. It was hard to hear. Kayzee spoke very softly. She kept her eyes down, and it made Crista feel a little uncomfortable. She's probably just really shy, Crista thought.

They talked about sports and school and Kayzee's friends from Atlanta. As they got off the bus at their stop between Rock Road and Midway Drive, Crista got an idea. "Hey, want to go horseback riding this afternoon?" She looked at Jeff.

Jeff nodded. "Sure, that would be great."

Both kids looked at Kayzee. "How about you, Kayzee?" Crista asked. "Have you ever been horseback riding?"

Again, Kayzee didn't look into Crista's eyes. "No, I haven't," she said. "I think I'd better get on home."

"Well, we can walk you there, at least," Crista said. "My dad won't be home for hours. And I usually go to Jeff's anyway."

"Oh, you don't have to do that," Kayzee said.

"That's okay, we'd like to." Crista smiled. "If you want, we can go up and just see the horses. They're friendly."

"I'll have to ask my brother, Jamal," Kayzee said, for the first time making eye contact.

"Then let's go," Crista said.

They hurried up the road and soon came to Kayzee's cabin. It was one of the nicer ones, more like a house than a cabin, with white slatboard siding, green shuttered windows, and a small parking area out front. There were two trees on either side of the stone path down to the front door. Between the trees hung a crossbeam with a pair of moose antlers attached.

"Cool," Jeff said. "I always thought this was a cool house. Did your mom and dad buy it?"

"No, we're just renting," Kayzee said. She led them up to the front door. "I'll go in and ask my brother."

The door was locked. Kayzee started to take out her key, but suddenly the door opened. A tall young man stood there with a tank top on. He had long, thin arms and in his right hand, a can of beer. Crista didn't drop her jaw, but she was amazed. The drinking age in Pennsylvania was twenty-one. And she thought Kayzee had said her brother was in high school.

Jamal said, "Mom's got a list for you, Kay. So get to it." He nodded to Jeff and Crista.

"This is my brother, Jamal," Kayzee said with pride in her voice. "He plays football."

"Not right now," Jamal said. He took a sip of the beer. "Get to it, Kayzee."

"Um, is it okay if I go up and see some horses for a little while?" Kayzee asked. "I'll be back in..."

"Half an hour," Crista put in. "At the latest."

"You'll be in trouble with Mom, but it's okay by me," Jamal said. "Best be back real quick."

"I will."

Kayzee turned to Jeff and Crista. "Let me dump off my backpack and I'll be right out."

In a moment, Kayzee returned. She stepped out, shutting the door behind her. Crista decided not to say anything about Jamal drinking beer. She figured that was Mrs. Jackson's business.

They walked up the road toward the Wilkinses' farm. In ten minutes, they crossed the highway to the other side of Rock Road and began jogging. When they reached the farm, they saw Mr. Wilkins's truck sitting in the front yard.

Crista spotted Mr. Wilkins in his overalls at the barn. Crista introduced Kayzee to him, and then they all went in and nuzzled the horses. Betsarama, a brown mare, was especially friendly. Kayzee immediately liked her and said so.

"I usually ride her when we ride," Crista said, "but I'll be glad to take Lukas or Brownie. Jeff usually rides Thunder."

"He's really big," Kayzee said. "I think he's too high for me."

"You want to get up on Betsarama?" Jeff asked.

Mr. Wilkins was smoking his pipe and cleaning out the stalls. "You kids want to ride?"

"No, we don't have time," Crista said. "Kayzee has to get back. But we could just take Betsarama out and get her up bareback."

"Would you?" Kayzee exclaimed. Her shyness seemed to be fading.

Mr. Wilkins slid a bridle over Betsarama's head and led her out of the stall. "Just bareback?" he asked.

"Sure," Crista replied. She looked at Kayzee. "We don't really have time for a whole saddle. But you can just jump up. Here, I'll help you." She made a step by linking her two hands together, lacing the fingers. "Put your left foot in my hands and I'll shoot you up."

Kayzee put her foot in place and suddenly she was mounted. "Ooh, this is great."

"Awesome," Jeff said.

"Radical," Crista added.

"We just say, smokin'," Kayzee said with a laugh.

Everyone chuckled.

Crista explained to Kayzee how to dismount, and a second later she was on the ground.

"Maybe tomorrow we'll go for a ride," Kayzee said.

"Smokin'," Jeff nodded his head.

Everyone laughed again.

"Thanks, Mr. Wilkins," they all called as they headed down the road. They soon reached the highway, where they crossed and hurried down to Rock Road. As they passed Jeff's house, Crista and Jeff pointed it out. Next they reached Crista's house, and Crista dropped off her backpack on the front stoop. Then she let out the two dogs, Rontu and Tigger, and they joined the little troop as they continued their walk. When they neared Midway Drive, they cut in through the trees at the end of the curve on Rock Road. They came out through the pines and stepped onto the dirt and rock path.

"I can go the rest of the way," Kayzee said.

"No, we'll walk you. We have time," Crista said.

They started down the road. A second later, Crista heard something whiz over her head.

"What was that?" She looked around.

"A rock!" Jeff said. "Duck!"

Two more rocks ripped across their path. Jeff ran to the edge of the road. "I see them!"

There was a shout, and Crista thought she heard someone yell an ugly word. But she wasn't sure.

Jeff ran further. He looked both ways. The two dogs bounded along behind him, barking.

"Who was it?" Crista called to Jeff.

"I couldn't tell," Jeff yelled back.

"What's going on?" Crista said. She called Rontu and Tigger to come back over. She didn't want one of them hit by a rock, either.

"Let's hurry up and get home," Kayzee said as Jeff and the dogs joined them again.

They all jogged up the road toward Kayzee's house.

"Who lives up this way?" Jeff asked as they ran. "I mean, who would throw rocks at us?"

"Danny Kluziewski lives down the next road,"

Crista said as she ran.

"Yeah," Jeff said.

Kayzee's eyes had a frightened look to them. She ran with the other two, but Crista could tell she was really scared. When they reached her house, she went right in.

"How are you guys going to get home?" Kayzee asked. "It's not safe out there."

"We'll be okay," Crista said at the door. "We can walk home."

"Are you sure?" Kayzee's eyes were doubtful.

"Yeah," Jeff answered with a grim look on his face.

He and Crista started off. When they were out of earshot of Kayzee's house, she said, "Did you hear what they said?"

"You mean the...the n-word?"

"Yeah."

"Yeah, I did."

"I wonder how Kayzee felt."

Jeff shook his head. "What a great introduction to Pennsylvania."

·3·

Ready for a Ride

That night Crista was sitting in the living room doing her homework when the phone rang. Dr. Mayfield answered it.

"Crista didn't say anything to me about it," she heard her father say. "Would you like to talk to her?" Crista looked up and her father held out the phone. "It's Mrs. Jackson. She wants to talk to you about something that happened today with her daughter, Kayzee. Did someone throw a rock at you?"

Crista nodded. "And they shouted out a word, too."

"What word?"

"You know, the bad word people use for black people."

Dr. Mayfield grimaced. "I would never have thought that would happen around here." He handed Crista the phone.

"Hi, this is Crista," Crista said into the receiver.

Mrs. Jackson's clear, resonant voice responded. "I'm very glad you were with Kayzee when this incident happened, Crista. You sound like a real friend."

"Kayzee's very nice, Mrs. Jackson."

"I understand she won a race at school today," Mrs. Jackson continued.

"Yes. We have these races every now and then. And Kayzee was first, with both boys and girls."

"And there are no other African-Americans in your class?"

"No, ma'am. In fact, Kayzee's the first African-American I ever knew."

Mrs. Jackson laughed softly. "Well, it's good of you to say that. But I'm concerned. Do you think these boys who threw the stones could have been in the class? Possibly the ones she beat in the race?"

"It's possible. We didn't see them up close. But Danny Kluziewski does live around here."

"I'd like to ask you and your friend, Jeff, a favor. Would you meet Kayzee at the bus stop each day, and then when she gets off, make sure she gets home okay?"

Crista glanced at her father who was listening to her side of the conversation. When he mouthed, "Is everything okay?" she mouthed back, "Yes. Don't worry about it." She said to Mrs. Jackson, "I'll be glad to."

"Thank you, Crista. I hope I meet you at school soon."

"You will."

"Bye-bye."

"Tell Kayzee I said hello."

"I will."

Crista hung up. Her father said, "What's going on?"

Crista explained what had happened that afternoon. Her father shook his head. "There is an element up here in this area that doesn't want any intruders. They might regard black people as intruders."

"But why? They're just people."

Her father sat down, raised his eyebrows, and shook his head again. "Some people don't see it that way. They see black people as troublemakers. They think every black person is like the gang kids we read about in the newspapers. We know they're not, but..."

"Kayzee did say that they came up here because Jamal was getting in with the wrong group," Crista interrupted.

"Who's Jamal?"

"Her brother." Crista walked toward the hallway into the kitchen. "I'm going to make dinner."

"What is it?"

"Stuffed peppers."

"That sounds good." Her father looked down at his magazine and began reading. Crista went into the kitchen to start supper. She couldn't get the stone-throwing incident out of her mind. Why did people act like that? Couldn't they get to know someone like Kayzee and find out she was a nice person before throwing stones at her?

Then another thought struck Crista: What if the stones weren't for Kayzee? What if they were meant for Crista and Jeff because they were Kayzee's friends?

She frowned as she stuffed the pepper with hamburger and cooked rice in a tomato sauce. "What if's" sped through her mind. What if people got mad at her because she liked Kayzee and the Jacksons? What if kids at school formed cliques, and she was left out? What if this whole thing got a great deal worse?

"No," she said as she shook her head. "That won't happen. Most of the kids at school are decent types. They wouldn't act like that."

But she didn't know whether she believed it.

When Saturday came, Crista ran through her chores early. She and Jeff had invited Kayzee to go horseback riding, and she wanted to get going as soon as possible. She got the wash done, or at least started in the washer and dryer, cleaned up after breakfast, made the beds, and stacked wood by the fireplace.

Her father had left early, at seven-thirty, for rounds at the hospital. He had three patients who were about to give birth, and two of them had called in the night saying they were experiencing pains. The hospital phoned early in the morning and told him they'd both come in and were definitely in labor. Crista always wondered what it must be like to deliver so many babies. It had to be really neat. But her father was very quiet and rarely said anything about it. Crista had seen one of her good friends, Nadine Semms, give birth to twins that winter. It had been a special moment for her father because they had been the first babies he had delivered since Crista's mother had died over a year ago. Because of the experience with Nadine, he'd gone back to being an obstetrician.

Crista finished her chores. At nine-fifteen she called Jeff. He wasn't even up yet. Jeff's grandmother said, "That boy could sleep through an atom bomb!"

"Well, get him up," Crista laughed. "We're supposed to go riding."

"Okay, honey. But if he yells at you, don't blame me."

Jeff came to the phone. His voice was husky and throaty, even a little gravelly, as if he had fuzz all over his tongue.

"Remember, we're going riding?" Crista asked.

"Yeah, but this early?"

"It's nine-fifteen, dodo-brain!" Crista exclaimed. "What—are you going to sleep your life away?"

"Sleeping is fun," Jeff countered.

"We're going riding, Jeff, not sleeping. Now are you coming or not?"

"Yeah, I'm coming."

"Then get ready."

"Aye, aye, sir."

Crista laughed. "I'll call Kayzee and let her know we're coming over. Shoot for ten o'clock, okay?"

"Yes, master." Jeff faked a robotic voice. "I will do exactly as you say, master."

Crista hung up. She pulled on her riding boots and got out her buckskin jacket with the little dangly pieces of leather along the sleeves and shoulders. It had been a present from her dad, but she hadn't worn it much yet. She didn't want to mess it up.

Jeff's knock at her door came at precisely five after ten, so Crista decided not to rail at him for being late. He was always late anyway, so what did she expect? They both traipsed up the road with Rontu and Tigger trotting along next to them.

"Watch out for stone-throwers," Jeff cautioned.

"I'm watching," Crista replied. "I hope that was the end of it."

"Probably. People get used to things. It's the sudden changes they don't like."

"Have you ever been prejudiced?" Crista asked. "I mean, you used to live in the city." Jeff had moved to Lake Wallenpaupack in the winter after his parents split up. He had lived in Philadelphia, but his mother didn't feel she could watch out for him in the big city. And Jeff rarely saw his father. The man had simply disappeared for months at first, and it made Jeff very angry. But as he settled into life on the lake with his grandparents, he and Crista became best friends, and he seemed to lose that angry edge. Because Crista had lost her mother, he felt as if she were a kindred spirit. She understood things about life that other kids didn't. Secretly, Crista sometimes thought of Jeff as her boyfriend. But they were only in sixth grade. They'd never kissed, held hands, or even gone out on a date—even though they did a lot of things together.

They reached Midway Drive and soon were knocking at the door of Kayzee's house. Mrs. Jackson answered. She was a pretty woman, slim, with creamy brown skin like her daughter's. She wore jeans and a flannel shirt. At school, she always wore a nurse's outfit and had a stethoscope around her neck. But today she looked like anyone else's mom: neat, casual, friendly, and ready for work around the house.

"So you're Crista, and I guess this is Jeff," Mrs. Jackson said immediately upon opening the door. "And these are your two dogs."

"Rontu and Tigger. The big one's Rontu," Crista answered. Rontu was a milky-white Great Dane. Tigger was a little Shelty with only one eye. The other one had been gouged out in a fight, or so Crista presumed. She had rescued both dogs from a hard life alone in the woods the previous winter.

Mrs. Jackson invited them in. The house had a front living room and dining room, with a kitchen in the back. Kayzee had told Crista there was one master bedroom downstairs, and three smaller bedrooms upstairs. Beyond the kitchen was a little den and a porch in the back.

"Sit down, sit down," Mrs. Jackson said as Kayzee joined them. "Would you all like a hot chocolate?"

"No, we just had breakfast," Crista said.

But Jeff piped up, "Yeah, I'll have one."

Crista frowned. "His stomach is a bottomless pit!"

"It is not!" Jeff argued, but he grinned. Mrs. Jackson brought him a steaming cup of the hot brown liquid.

Kayzee had dressed in jeans and a blue shirt with a cross-stitched design on the collars and the pockets.

"Nice shirt," Crista said. "Did your mom do it?"

"No, I did," Kayzee answered. She smiled. "Like it?"

"Yeah, it looks good," Jeff replied between sips. "I made one for Crista once like that."

"You did not!" Crista cried.

"Just wanted to see if she was still awake." He grinned slyly at Kayzee. "She gets up so early these days that she nods off about ten-fifteen."

Crista shook her head. "I do not! Anyway, you ready to go, Kayzee?"

"I guess," Kayzee said. "I'm kind of nervous." She pulled on her coat. "I like your jacket, Crista."

"Yeah, she chased the girl a couple miles for it!" Jeff said with a chuckle.

Crista shook her head and rolled her eyes. "I see you're in a good mood." She turned to Kayzee. She was setting her braids up behind her head with a large leather barrette. Crista said, "My dad bought it for me. This is the first time I've really worn it."

"Except for sleeping in it day and night," Jeff said, interrupting.

"Good grief, will you can it with the jokes!" Crista said. "Man, we're going to have to tie you down."

Jeff finished the hot chocolate. "Good stuff, Mrs. Jackson. You make the best."

"Why thank you, Jeff," Mrs. Jackson said. "I'm sure that's a real compliment coming from you."

She smiled cryptically and Crista said, "Yeah, I've never gotten one good compliment out of him for my cooking. And he eats over all the time."

"Oh, I say nice stuff to you," Jeff protested.

"Like when?"

"Last February 6, at five p.m. I said, 'I can dig on it.'"

"Yeah, right."

Everyone laughed.

Kayzee stood by the door. "Well, ready to go?"

Crista and Jeff stood. "This is going to be a great time," Jeff said. "I hope you're really ready."

"I don't know," Kayzee said, "but I'm willing to try." She gave her mom a kiss. "I'll be back in—what —a couple of hours?"

"After lunch," Crista said. "No later than two or so."

"All right. Have fun," Mrs. Jackson said.

The three kids stepped out of the house. The two

dogs, who had been waiting on the front stoop, jumped up. Rontu gave Kayzee a friendly sniff and then all of them were off.

"I've got my slingshot," Jeff said. "In case of attack by rock."

"I hope that doesn't happen again," Crista said.

"Let's not talk about it." Kayzee frowned. "It gives me the shakes."

They all headed down the road and soon were out at the highway. No one appeared in the woods. No rocks were thrown. But Crista still felt a little flutter in her heart as they walked along.

·4·
Into the Woods

Mr. Wilkins held Betsarama's bridle as Kayzee put her foot in a stirrup. "Take it slow now, honey. You don't need to gallop your first time out. Hear that, kids?"

"Of course," Jeff said. "I'm going to fly. But Crista will walk all the way."

"Oh, I can try to go faster than a walk," Kayzee said boldly.

"Take it one step at a time," Crista said. "That's all I ask for."

"You got it!" Kayzee agreed enthusiastically. She threw her right leg over the saddle, then stuck her feet in the stirrups. Crista was already mounted on Lukas, and Jeff was climbing aboard Thunder. Mr. Wilkins handed Kayzee the reins.

"Crista's explained it all to you? How to go right and left?" he asked.

"Yes," Kayzee said. She swished the reins to the right and the horse's head came around. Then she did the same to the left.

"Just give her a little kick and she'll be off. You

know how to stop?" Mr. Wilkins said again.

"Just pull back like this," Kayzee answered. She demonstrated.

"Sounds like she's all checked out and ready to roll," Mr. Wilkins said. He puffed on his pipe. "All right. Be careful. And don't take no wooden nickels."

Crista led them out of the barn. When they reached the road, Kayzee said, "What was that about wooden nickels?"

"Something Mr. Wilkins says," Crista explained. "An old person's expression."

"Oh," Kayzee said. "Can we trot now?"

"Already?"

"Yeah!"

"Okay, give her a little kick."

Suddenly, Crista and Kayzee were in a trot. Jeff had to kick Thunder hard to catch up. They wound on down the road, bouncing in the trot like little bubbles leaping out of a blow ring. As they came to the road into the trees, Crista told Jeff, "If you want to go on ahead of us, be my guest."

"No, I'll stick with you," Jeff said. He gestured to his slingshot dangling from his back pocket. "In case of attack," he whispered. Kayzee didn't hear him.

"In Atlanta," Kayzee said, "we hardly had any woods. But up here, everything is woods."

"Goes on for miles," Crista said. "Sometime maybe we can take a camping trip. I just went on one last week with my dad and my cousin from

California." Crista told Kayzee about taking an overnight trip into the woods and running into a rabid husky. Kayzee's eyes were wide.

"I've heard about rabies," she said. "That's dangerous."

"You're telling me," Crista said. "I was terrified. But luckily we took care of it." She told the rest of the story as they reached the tee where the dump road joined their road.

"Down that way is the dump," Crista said, pointing to the left and stopping. The horses snorted and stamped their feet. In the cool air, their breath came in a slight mist. "We'll go there sometime, but today we're heading off to the right. I want you to meet one of my best friends of all time, Nadine Semms, and her twins, and her husband, Johnny."

"They live right out in the woods?" Kayzee asked.

"Like *Little House on the Prairie*," Crista said. "Come on."

They trotted down the road, and Kayzee shouted above the noise of the horses' hooves, "Can we go faster?"

"You sure are taking to this," Crista said. She peered at Jeff. He simply shrugged, gave Thunder a wallop, and bounded off into a canter.

"I don't want you to fall off," Crista warned. "Are you sure?"

"I feel pretty good. Trotting wasn't hard," Kayzee replied. "I think I can go faster."

"Okay, but hold on with your knees," Crista instructed. "Squeeze tight, and if you need to, grab the pommel. That's what I usually do if I feel myself slipping."

"What's after a trot?"

"Pacing, then canter, then gallop. We're not going to gallop." Crista shook her head. "You sure are adventurous."

"Born that way," Kayzee said. She gave Betsarama a kick. Immediately, the big brown horse jolted into a trot. Kayzee kicked harder, and the horse was into a lope and then a canter before Crista had even moved.

She shouted, "Go!" to Lukas, and the grey stallion leaped into a full canter. In a few seconds, Crista caught up to Kayzee, her hair whipping in the air behind her.

"Like it?" she shouted over the pounding of the horses' hooves.

"It's cool!" Kayzee yelled back. She was gripping the pommel, looking like any second she would fly off the saddle into the brambles. But she stayed on.

Soon, they streamed around the bend and the Semmses' cabin came into sight. Crista reined up on Lukas and Kayzee followed her lead. Jeff was already standing there, Thunder stamping his hooves, in the Semmses' front yard.

Nadine stood out on the porch with one of the twins in her arms, Johnny, Junior, judging by the color of the romper outfit he was wearing.

"Hi, kids," Nadine called as Crista and Kayzee trotted up. "Come on in, I've got the sandwiches ready."

"We're having lunch here," Crista said to Kayzee. She dismounted and then helped Kayzee jump down. They tied the horses to the rail on the porch in front of the cabin. Crista hurried over to Nadine. "This is Kayzee Jackson." She turned to Kayzee. "This is Nadine Semms, my best adult friend. And her little son, age five months, Johnny Semms, Junior."

Kayzee grinned and held out her hand. "Pleased to meet you," she said.

After shaking hands, Nadine led them into the house. "I presume you brought your appetite, Jeff Pallaci."

"Oh yeah!" Jeff said. "Ready for three of your BLTs. That's what we're having, isn't it?"

"Tomatoes and all," Nadine said. As she stepped inside, Johnny, Senior smiled at all of them. He sat at the rustic oaken table, holding the other twin, Fairlight.

"Hey," he said.

Crista introduced Kayzee to Johnny and Fairlight, who just gurgled and drooled onto Johnny's shoulder.

"Sit down, sit down," Nadine said. "Cokes everyone?"

"Fine by me," Jeff said. Crista and Kayzee nodded with approval.

They all sat down and, after a short grace, were soon chomping into their bacon, lettuce, and tomato sandwiches. Johnny, Senior chattered about his work at a local Jiffy Lube. He was going to make assistant manager, he said, if things continued as they were. That would mean an increase in salary, and it made Crista glad. Nadine and Johnny needed the money.

When they finished the meal, Nadine cleared the table. "So, Kayzee," she said. "Tell me about yourself."

Kayzee told Johnny, Senior and Nadine about Atlanta and most of the other things she'd already told Crista and Jeff. The hour passed quickly, and soon it was time to go.

Kayzee and Jeff went out first. Before Crista stepped out, Nadine whispered, "I like your new friend."

"Yeah, she's great," Crista said. "But I'm worried."

"What about?"

Crista quickly told her about the rock incident.

"That's horrible," Nadine said.

"Yeah," Johnny said, "we had stuff like that in our high school. The blacks and the whites were always at it."

"What did you do?" Crista asked.

"We moved up here," Johnny said with a shrug.

"I'm afraid we can't do that," Crista said. "We're already here."

"Welcome to the real world," Nadine said. "I hope everything works out okay for you and Kayzee."

"It will," Crista said. She stepped out into the sunlight. Jeff and Kayzee were already mounted.

"Hey," Nadine called as Crista got on her horse, "how come Lindy didn't come with you today?"

"Lindy!" Crista cried. "I forgot all about Lindy!" Lindy was a second-grader who Crista tutored and sometimes babysat. She often joined Jeff and Crista on their horseback rides.

Jeff looked at her. "Uh oh!"

·5·
Caught!

"Well, we just don't tell her," Crista said. "What she doesn't know won't hurt her."

The three kids trotted back toward Mr. Wilkins's farm. On the way they passed Lindy's house. Lindy came running out as they went by.

"Hey," Lindy called. "Hi, everybody."

Crista reined in Lukas. "We were just out riding. This is Kayzee Jackson. Lindy Helstrom."

Lindy performed a deft curtsy. "You could have invited me," she said.

"We forgot," Crista said honestly. "I'm really sorry, Lindy. We just got going and forgot."

"Don't forget next time." Lindy gave her a big smile.

The horses all stood in the middle of the road panting and chuffing and snorting. Lindy waved. "Nice meeting you, Kayzee. See you later. I'm making cookies with my mom."

"Save some for us," Crista called as Lindy ran inside.

"Nice little kid," Kayzee said when Lindy was

gone. Crista turned Lukas around, and they all headed up the road. In a few minutes, they pulled into the barn and dismounted. Crista showed Kayzee how to take the saddles and reins off and to brush down the horses. When they were done, they all thanked Mr. Wilkins and went out to the main road. The three of them talked about Lindy, Nadine, the twins, and other things.

They walked down the highway and, in another minute, they cut into the trees and caught Rock Road. They hurried past Jeff's house and then Crista's. Finally, they reached Midway Drive. As they walked toward Kayzee's house, they noticed a truck parked on the left side. It was a ramshackle gray Ford. In the back window, Crista could see a gunrack with two rifles stretched across it. Smoke sifted into the air out of the right-hand window. The man was just sitting there.

The kids passed by on the far side of the street. Crista whispered, "Don't look at him now. We'll get to the house and look out the windows."

As they passed the truck and reached Kayzee's house, the man suddenly turned the ignition key and the engine turned over. A moment later, it roared. Smoke billowed out behind it. The man threw the truck into gear and with a whirring of wheels sped in front of the kids. As he went by, the man scrutinized all three of them standing there. Then the wheels spun again, and the truck wheeled by in a cloud of dust.

"I wonder what he's doing," Kayzee said with a little shiver.

"I got the license plate," Crista said. "We can report him to the police if he comes around again. He doesn't live here, does he, Kayzee?"

Kayzee shook her head. "I don't know. I never saw him before."

"Let's tell your mom," Crista said. "This is getting creepy."

"Do you think he was watching our house?" Kayzee asked.

"Why would he do that in plain daylight?" Jeff said. "He'd be in a perfect position to get caught. I don't think so."

"Maybe it was intimidation," Crista suggested.

"What's that?" Jeff asked.

"You know, making people feel scared," she said. She looked at Kayzee. "It'll be okay. If we have to, we'll just call the police. I think we should tell your mother, and you'll have to be on the lookout if he shows up again."

They went inside and told Mrs. Jackson. She said she'd be watching, but she didn't think they should jump to conclusions. "Not yet anyway," she assured them.

Crista hoped Mrs. Jackson was right.

Crista went to church on Sunday with her father and, to her surprise, Kayzee, her mother, and her two brothers were there, too. Crista introduced her father to the Jackson family.

"Crista's told me a lot about you all," Dr. Mayfield said, shaking hands with Mrs. Jackson and Jamal. "Welcome to the community. I hear you didn't get such a warm reception, though."

"We're not worried," Mrs. Jackson commented. "We'll be careful, but I think people will be friendly in the long run. Once they see we're decent peace-loving folks."

Dr. Mayfield smiled. "Would you all like to go with us to get a bite to eat? Crista and I usually hit the Jolly Roger for burgers and fries after church."

Mrs. Jackson glanced around at her children. Kayzee said, "Can we, Mama, please?"

"I guess," Mrs. Jackson finally said.

Pastor Matthews said hello at the door and expressed hope that the Jackson family would be back. He shook hands with all of them.

Lunch at the Jolly Roger was uneventful, but Crista did notice several people turn around and look long and hard at the newcomers. She immediately felt angry. Why did people have to act like black people in the area were aliens? After all, the main cities of Pennsylvania all had their share of people from different cultures. She didn't say anything to Kayzee, though, and as they ate their hamburgers, everyone settled down for a friendly meal and chat.

Crista didn't see Kayzee again until the next morning at the bus stop. They sat together with Jeff behind them, cracking jokes. School went along as usual until gym. Mr. Rader chose Danny Kluziewski and Brad Holmes as captains for the softball teams. Jeff was picked second and Crista was picked fifth but Kayzee was the very last one picked. And Brad seemed a little reluctant to take her. It made Crista angry, but again she decided people just needed to get to know Kayzee, and then all would be well.

At the end of gym, Crista walked over to Mr. Rader and talked to him about Kayzee being chosen last. He said, "I know, I didn't like it either. Maybe next time we'll just count off."

"That might be better," Crista agreed. "Until Kayzee gets a chance to prove herself." Kayzee had gotten two hits in the game and made one nice catch. She was obviously athletic.

"I think after today everyone will be wanting her on their team," Mr. Rader said. "Don't worry about it, Crista. Things like this usually iron themselves out."

Crista ran in and took her seat at the bell. She didn't say anything to Jeff or Kayzee about her talk with Mr. Rader.

That afternoon when Crista and Jeff walked Kayzee home, there was a police car sitting in front of Kayzee's house. Mrs. Jackson pulled up in her white Camry just as they arrived. She said, "Kayzee, you'll have to come inside. Crista and Jeff, I'm sorry. You'd better get on home." Her face looked dark with anxiety.

Crista and Jeff hurried home. Crista invited him in for a Coke, hoping that Kayzee would call and tell her what on earth was going on.

Sure enough, half an hour later, the phone rang.

"The Mayfield residence," Crista said, answering.

"Crista, this is Kayzee," the voice said.

"What on earth happened?"

"Jamal. He was caught selling firecrackers to boys in the high school," Kayzee said, her voice trembling. "Mom has to go down to the police station to get him. It's big trouble. He had cherry bombs, M-80s, and whole strings of Black Cats. He was always messing with them down at home."

"What was he selling firecrackers for?"

"Oh, you know, he's always coming up with something." Kayzee sighed. "That's why we moved up here, to get away from it. And now it looks like Jamal brought it with him."

"Brought what?"

"Trouble."

"Do you want me to call my dad?" Crista said. "He knows all the police. He might be able to help."

"No, Mom's going to take care of it. She left me here with Lukie."

"This is really awful, Zee," Crista said impulsively.

"Wow," Kayzee said, "kids in Atlanta used to call me Zee. And Kay. And other stuff."

"Like what?"

Kayzee laughed. "The Flash."

Crista laughed in response. "Good one." A second later, Crista turned serious again. "I mean, you've only been here a week and a half, Zee. It's ridiculous your brother selling firecrackers."

"I know. Mom is furious at Jamal. She also found out about him drinking beer. He had hidden some in his room."

Crista sighed. "Is there anything I can do?"

"Just pray for my brother, that's all. I better go."

When she hung up, Crista told Jeff about everything. He whistled. "Firecrackers are illegal up here."

"No kidding."

"And cherry bombs and M-80s. They're dangerous. Even though I wouldn't mind having some. Maybe Jamal will sell me some!"

"Don't talk like that, Jeff!" Crista exclaimed. "The Jacksons have enough trouble."

"Yeah, I shouldn't crack jokes."

"What can we do?"

Jeff looked at her unhappily. "I don't know. I guess just hope things don't get worse."

·6·
Pictures for Sale

The next day there was an article in the local paper on the front page. The headline read, "Youth Caught Selling Fireworks." There was a picture of Jamal and some statements from the police as well as Mrs. Jackson. She had said, "Jamal is generally a good boy. I don't know what's gotten into his mind about this, but this is the end of it. You can be sure of that." There had been bail of $200, and Jamal was charged as an adult. It was a complete mess.

At the bus stop, Kayzee said to Crista and Jeff confidentially, "Down in Atlanta a lot of kids get into trouble. But up here, it's just one. And it's big news. Something like this wouldn't even be in the papers in Atlanta. I don't know how he got caught so easily."

"There's an informer, I bet," Crista said. "One of the boys who was buying ratted on Jamal."

"Maybe," Kayzee said. "But that's to be expected. Jamal is just stupid. And now he's in big trouble. Serves him right."

Crista exhaled breathily with frustration. "And

with all the other stuff, this is terrible."

On the bus, Crista pulled out a drawing pad. She began to absently draw a picture of Rontu with a pencil. Kayzee watched as the lines flowed into the outline of a dog and then a picture.

"You're really good," Kayzee commented.

"It's my main talent," Crista said. "Say, want me to do a picture of you?"

"That would be great," Kayzee smiled. "But let me sit on the other side of you. My left side is my best profile."

Crista laughed as they switched seats. As the bus smoothly rolled along the highway, she drew in the lines of Kayzee's profile. Then a nose appeared and eyebrows, eyes, eyelids, lips, a chin. Kayzee stared in fascination. "I never saw anyone draw like that."

"Sometimes I go to the strip mall downtown and do caricatures. Would you like to come? We can earn some money. If you advertise, I'll give you half of what I make."

"Really? What do I have to do?"

"Just go through the mall with a sign and some pictures. Tell people where to go."

"I wouldn't mind telling some people where to go."

Crista laughed and Kayzee chuckled. "No, really, would you do it?" Crista asked. "We can go down there this Saturday."

"Great idea. Now finish the drawing."

Crista drew quickly. The lines and contours of

Kayzee's face all fell into place. Crista gave it just the right shading. As the bus pulled into the schoolyard, Crista finished. Kayzee stared at the result.

"It's marvelous," she said. "You could be a portrait painter."

"Maybe one day. I'm good with pencils and charcoal. But I've never tried watercolors. I've done a little in oils, but they're much harder. You have to learn how to mix the paints and that's tough. I'm not good at it yet. But it's fun."

As Kayzee oohed and aahed over the painting, Crista got an idea. "Would you like me to do a picture of each member of your family? For a little collage?"

"Oh, I'm sure we couldn't afford it."

"I wouldn't charge you anything. It would be fun. I could do a group portrait, or just one of each of you. In charcoal, or in chalk, whichever you want."

"Wow!" Kayzee said. "I'll tell my mom. I'm sure she'd go for it."

That Saturday, Crista set up her easel with a box of chalks on the little strip mall on the far side of Hawley. Crista did a caricature of Kayzee first, to use as an advertisement.

She sat Kayzee down, had her display her profile, and then Crista began to draw. She homed in right away on Kayzee's lush brown cheeks and high cheekbones. She gave her a pert little nose and bright red lips. She dressed Kayzee up to look like a model, then after finishing the face, she drew in a little mini-caricature of the body of a model strutting down a runway displaying a beautiful new gown. Crista drew a little sign to the right of Kayzee's face, "Models, Inc." and also drew in a bathing suit, a tennis outfit, and riding togs as it might be in a catalog.

Kayzee was delighted. "It's so beautiful," she said. "I'm not anywhere that beautiful."

"Sure you are," Crista said. "Now go out and drum me up some business."

Kayzee had a placard that read, "Crista Mayfield, Caricature Artist," and held the picture of herself. Then she walked up and down the full length of the mall, telling people where to have their portraits drawn.

Soon, Crista had a few customers. She did a little boy, who liked soccer, and his mother, who wanted to grill a steak that night.

Next, an old farmer with deep lines in his face was persuaded by his wife to sit for a portrait. And then the woman herself sat. Crista gave them both a twinkle in the eye and sharp chins with deep, wrinkly smiles. It was perfect. Both of them paid their ten dollars without a blink.

As soon as Crista would finish a portrait, Kayzee would bring her another customer. In the afternoon, Mr. and Mrs. Wilkins came by and watched for a while. They both commented on how nice

Crista made everyone look. "Better than they do look," Mr. Wilkins whispered. Mrs. Wilkins nudged him in the side and frowned.

Later, Dr. Mayfield stopped by to pick Crista and Kayzee up but Crista still had two people lined up to be drawn. He walked down to a small restaurant on the corner to have a coffee.

When the day was over, Crista had made a hundred and forty dollars. She gave seventy to Kayzee, and Kayzee was amazed. "I never had that much money before in my life."

"Well, this was a particularly good day," Crista admitted. "I couldn't have done it without you."

They left the easel standing with Kayzee's picture on it while they both went to the local clothing shop to pick out something for themselves.

"You could be rich, Crista," Kayzee said. "I mean, you made a hundred and forty dollars in what—five hours? That's incredible!"

"It doesn't always go this well," Crista reminded her. "Some Saturdays I've sat there all day and didn't have one single customer!"

They found a couple of nice shirts in the clothing store and came out wearing two western hats. Crista felt as if she'd made a lifelong friend that day. Kayzee was really opening up.

When they came back to the easel, they were shocked at what they found. Someone had taken charcoal and scribbled right over the picture of Kayzee. In the bottom corner, they had scrawled,

"Ugly!"

Crista was struck with anger and fear. "Let's find out if someone saw who did this."

They both went into the little smoke shop opposite where Crista had set up the easel. But no one inside had seen anything. Whoever had done it, had gotten away with it.

"I'll do another picture," Crista said, trying to make Kayzee feel better. "They're easy."

"But I liked this one." Kayzee's lower lip trembled.

"Sit down. Let's do this right away."

Crista drew another portrait, but Kayzee began crying. "Who is doing this, Crista, who?"

"I don't know," Crista said. "But we're going to find out."

She finished the portrait in another ten minutes. When she was done, Kayzee said, "Can you fix the other one, too?"

"I'll try," Crista said. "But I don't know. I'll have to take it home."

"Please. I love them both. Thanks, Crista."

"We're going to find out who's doing this, Kayzee. You'll see."

"I hope. I really want to give him a word or two."

·7·

A Mysterious Truck

At the bus stop the next Monday, Jeff said, "Say, want to go fishing this afternoon? That might be fun and it would get your minds off this stuff."

Crista nodded. "Yeah, the lake is full of fish, and this time of year there aren't many people out there. We might land a pickerel or a northern pike."

"I'll just settle for some bass," Jeff said. "How about it, Kayzee?"

The big yellow bus pulled up.

"I'll think about it," Kayzee said. It was obvious she was still pretty upset.

"Come on, it'll calm you. And it's fun." Jeff led them onto the bus. "I say we catch our supper. There's nothing like good eating when it comes to fresh caught bass."

"After I do my homework," Kayzee said, taking a seat.

"Before," Jeff persisted. "You can do your homework at night."

"We'll see what happens today, Jeff," Crista came to Kayzee's rescue, "and decide on our way home.

Maybe Lindy can join us, too."

The bus was quiet as they drove to school. But when they reached the schoolyard, as the kids filed off, Crista thought she heard someone whisper a nasty word about black people again. She glanced at Jeff, but he didn't seem to have noticed. Kayzee was chattering about something else, so Crista decided to ignore it.

This time at gym, Mr. Rader had everyone count off for softball teams and, though some boys grumbled, it worked okay. Kayzee played well in softball and was fast becoming the best girl player. Crista had never been very good at catching, but she could hit and usually got on base several times. Jeff was a natural athlete and always did well.

After school that afternoon, Jeff, Crista, Kayzee, and Lindy set out to go fishing. They headed for the point. It was a jut of land out into the cove where Crista's house as well as the others were situated. It was good for fishing, and Jeff had pulled in many sunfish, bass, and even a perch or two over the last few weeks.

Crista let Kayzee use her mother's fishing rod, a spin cast that was long and limber. Kayzee learned how to cast quickly. Crista was constantly amazed at how fast Kayzee picked things up. Soon, Lindy's pole bent with signs of a big one.

She reeled it in and an eight-inch sunny hung from the line. Lindy refused to take it off, so Crista helped her. They put the sunny on a gill line tied to a stake.

Crista was next and reeled in a small bass. She threw him back. Then Jeff pulled in a seven-inch bluegill. He was a "keeper," and a second fish was added to the gill line. Lindy pulled in another sunfish that was too small. Kayzee meanwhile had walked a ways down the beach and still had caught nothing. Jeff suggested she try a new worm.

After making the adjustment, Kayzee came up with her first catch: a perch, about nine inches long. She was excited.

The kids yammered and caught the afternoon away until they had a string of eight fish, enough for quite a feast.

As Jeff put the last fish on the gill line, Crista heard a stick crack in the woods behind them. She whipped around and peered into the trees. She couldn't see anything, but she was sure she'd heard a branch crack.

"Maybe it was just an old branch falling," Jeff volunteered.

Crista walked up closer to the woods. Her heart was beating hard. Everyone joined her and looked, but nothing moved. The woods were dark and thick, full of underbrush. Anyone in there would have a hard time walking. But there was a little road not far to the right.

"Let's just go," Jeff suggested. "We've caught enough fish for one day."

They all gathered up their gear.

Then Lindy heard another crack.

"I know it was a stick this time!" she exclaimed.

The kids pulled all their gear together and walked close to the woods, looking for the road down to the point. A moment later, they heard a truck roar and, in a puff of smoke, a gray ramshackle truck disappeared deep into the woods. Everyone saw it this time. It looked like the same truck that had been sitting near Kayzee's house.

"Someone was watching us," Crista said uneasily.

"We'd better get home." Jeff's voice was scratchy.

"What is it?" Lindy asked. She knew nothing of the rock throwing incident, or of what had happened to Jamal.

"It looked like a truck we saw at Kayzee's house a few days ago," Jeff commented.

"Let's get home. I'm calling the police," Crista said.

"And what will we tell them?" Kayzee asked.

"That a man was watching us."

"Can we prove that?" Kayzee asked again. "I mean, we don't really know for sure."

Crista shook her head. "I wrote down that license number. I'm going to report him."

·8·

It Takes Two

At home, Crista dialed the local police station. When a woman answered, Crista said, "I'd like to report a suspicious character."

The female officer asked for a name and address and then said, "Can you describe the situation for me?"

"Yes," Crista said. "Three days ago, I and my friends Jeff and Kayzee were walking up Midway Drive when we passed this ramshackle gray truck. It had two guns in the gunrack above the rear window. We passed the truck, and when we got by, the person inside suddenly started it and roared away. He stared at us as he went by. Then today, the three of us and another friend named Lindy Helstrom were fishing and we thought someone was watching us. Sure enough, we walked near the woods, looked in, and saw this same truck. He roared away as before. We think he's following us."

"Do you have a license plate number or anything like that?" the woman asked.

"Yes." Crista gave her the numbers.

"All right, we'll check it out. How old are you?"

"Twelve."

"Your parents' names?"

Crista gave her father's name.

"Okay, we'll have an officer investigate."

"Will you let us know what happens?"

"Yes. We'll contact you."

"Thank you."

Crista breathed a sigh of relief. When she hung up, she said to the other three, "All right, now things are in motion. We're going to find out who this person is and what he's up to."

There was no answer from the police that afternoon or evening. The next morning, Crista met Jeff and Kayzee at the bus stop. After they got on the bus and sat down, they remained quiet for the ride down the road. They picked up Lindy at the next stop, and she sat down with Jeff.

"Did the police call?" she asked right away.

"Nothing," Crista said.

Kayzee said, "I wish this would all just go away."

"So do I," Jeff replied. "Let's just be cool and not discuss it. It's all too weird for me."

At school, things went quietly along until lunch. Crista and Jeff sat with Kayzee and some other friends at a table. Halfway through lunch, a girl named Tonya Murphy went by their table with a tray in her hands. As she passed Kayzee, she tripped, dropping the tray in Kayzee's lap.

"How dare you trip me!" Tonya yelled. "You did that on purpose!"

"No, I didn't," Kayzee protested in amazement. "You just..."

Before Kayzee could finish, Tonya jerked her up and tried to hit her. Crista and Jeff jumped up. Jeff grabbed Tonya and pulled her away. She began screaming, "She tripped me. She ruined my lunch!"

Crista held Kayzee. "Just be calm," she said. "It was an accident. Tonya's overreacting."

"Overreacting?" Kayzee shouted, trying to pull away. "She tried to punch me!"

Two teachers were running over, trying to get to the two kids. Tonya jerked away from Jeff and got in a kick, and Kayzee kicked back. The whole table was a mess. Kids were up and shouting all over.

"Get her, Tonya!"

"Slug her!"

"Don't take that offa her, Tonya!"

"Mr. Simpson!" Crista cried to the teacher on lunch duty. She couldn't control Kayzee, and Jeff couldn't stop her. Some kids were using the n-word for Kayzee. It was complete turmoil.

Mr. Simpson reached the two fighting girls. He jumped in between them and held them off.

"All right, what's going on here?" he yelled.

Everyone began shouting at once.

He motioned to Mrs. James to grab Kayzee and he took Tonya. "We're going to the principal's office," he ordered. "Everyone back to their rooms. Immediately!"

Kids grumbled and shouted at one another.

Crista made her way slowly back to the classroom and waited. She was crying. Jeff sat next to her, whispering that it was all right, everything was going to be okay.

"How could this be happening?" Crista asked. "It's chaos! Just because Kayzee is black? That makes no sense."

Several kids sat looking at Crista and she said to Danny Kluziewski, "You've certainly made enough trouble, Danny!"

Mrs. Roberts rapped a ruler on her desk. "There will be quiet here now! Everyone in his or her seat. No talking!"

"But Mrs. Roberts..." Crista wailed.

"Crista, be quiet. I know Kayzee is your friend and..."

"And Tonya is ours," Danny Kluziewski butted in.

"Danny, be quiet. *Everyone* be quiet!" Mrs. Roberts said angrily. "There will be no more of this arguing in my class. Understood?"

No one answered. Crista glanced at Jeff, who gave her a little thumbs up. Suddenly the loudspeaker came on. It was Principal Burleson.

"Mrs. Roberts, I'm sending Tonya back to class along with my secretary. I'd like you to come to my office once they arrive."

A few minutes later, Tonya returned. Several of the kids cheered, but Mrs. Roberts stifled that immediately. The principal's secretary took her place in the front and Mrs. Roberts left.

A few minutes later, she returned, but Kayzee wasn't with her. Crista wondered where she was.

"Kayzee is down at the nurse's station," Mrs. Roberts said quietly as she walked to the front of the room. "Tonya, you will be sitting here a half-hour after school and writing on the board whatever I decide a hundred times. There will be no more fighting in this class. Kayzee has as much right to be here as any of you. Your actions today were wrong. They smacked of racism. Our society does not permit discrimination in any form. Do you understand what that means?"

When no one answered, Mrs. Roberts continued, "Our country guarantees the Bill of Rights, the right to vote, the right of free speech, the right to life, liberty, and the pursuit of happiness, the right to employment, and so on with no discrimination as to creed, religion, sex, national origin, or race. That means Kayzee gets the same rights all of you do. Anyone who attacks Kayzee or hurls bigoted epithets...uses racist, ugly words around here is in danger of suspension from school, and possible expulsion. I don't think your parents want that. Now when Kayzee comes back, we will all welcome her as a friend and an equal. I am very serious about this."

Everyone remained quiet. "Get out your composition notebooks," Mrs. Roberts instructed, "and write the statement that I put on the board fifty times over the next half-hour."

A moan of disgruntlement swept through the class, but Mrs. Roberts held up her hand. "I will hear no more of this. And if there's anymore fighting, that person or persons will go immediately to the principal. I don't care who started it. The principal will sort it out and pass out detentions."

She turned around and wrote on the board: "I will not discriminate against anyone on the basis of race, religion, creed, or national origin."

"Fifty times," she said again. "No kidding around."

Everyone opened their notebooks. Mrs. Roberts sat down and watched. No one said anything. Pencils began to scratch on paper.

·9·
Ugly Words

The last few periods that afternoon went by slowly, and it seemed everyone was jumpy. Kayzee came back to class after being away about half an hour. She didn't say anything to Crista or Jeff. But she looked scared and determined at the same time.

Filing out to the buses after school, Crista noticed a commotion in the parking lot. Some kids who normally walked to school crowded around a car.

"What is it?" Crista asked Jeff.

He craned his neck. "Come on," he said. "We have time."

They ran over to the lot. When they got there, Crista stared in horror at the side of Mrs. Jackson's car. Written on the white painted surface were stark red letters: "N---- go home!"

Kids talked excitedly until the custodian, Mr. Felix, came out to investigate. He immediately moved everyone out of the area and then went inside and found the principal.

Kayzee started crying.

"I can't believe this!" Crista said to Jeff, clenching her fists. "Why are people doing this? I just wish they'd come out and show themselves. I'd give them a piece of my mind."

Crista placed her arm around Kayzee's shoulders. "Come on, Zee, you don't need to see this."

Mrs. Jackson stalked outside with the principal. All the kids moved back and waited. Mrs. Jackson shook her head. The principal's face was red, and he whipped around, looking at the gathering. "Does anyone know who did this?"

No one answered.

"If one of you kids knows and you're not talking, you'll be in big trouble when the culprit is found," Mr. Burleson said, his face looking ruddy, almost purple with anger. "This is wrong, just dead wrong. And whoever is doing it will be punished severely."

A boy named Jesse Kingston raised his hand. "We were all inside since lunchtime, Mr. Burleson."

The principal stared at everyone with hard, burning eyes. "If anyone sees or learns anything, I want to know about it immediately."

He turned to Mrs. Jackson, who had her face in her hands. "Do you want me to call some people to come and get this paint off your car?"

"Please," Mrs. Jackson said. She looked like she was crying.

Kayzee and Lukie walked over and stood on either side of her. Then Crista joined them. Next Jeff came. Soon, several students had gathered around Mrs. Jackson to show their support.

Someone whistled from the parking lot. It was time to get on the buses. Crista said to Mrs. Jackson, "Would you like us to stay here with you, till they get the paint off your car?"

"No, Crista," Mrs. Jackson said. "You go home on the bus. Kayzee and Luke, you stay here with me." She headed toward the steps inside the school building. Kayzee and Luke followed. Crista and Jeff were left standing there, looking again at the car with its red lettering.

"It's wrong," Crista said. "People who do these kinds of things should be punished."

"And you'd be just the person to do the punishing," Jeff quipped.

"No jokes," Crista said, stalking back across the blacktop to the bus. "This is no time for jokes."

Jeff hurried after her. "I'm just trying to lighten it up, Crista."

"Don't!"

They took their seat on the bus, and Crista glared at Danny Kluziewski as he paraded on, looking proud and cocky as usual. She heard some of the boys talking in whispers in the back of the bus, and it made her all the more angry. She thought she ought to tell Mr. Burleson her suspicions about Danny and his friends. But she couldn't prove anything. She didn't want to be a tattletale and a rat for no reason. She would need proof.

When they arrived home, Jeff came into Crista's

house for a Coke. They drank in silence, sitting at the long counter in the kitchen. Jeff kept looking out the window. Crista felt frustrated and wanted to talk, but she didn't know what to say.

Finally, Jeff broke the silence. "This is getting serious," he said.

"That's for sure," Crista agreed. She took a sip of her Coke. "I'm going to call Kayzee."

"Good idea."

She walked over to the black rotary phone. After dialing the number, she listened to the ringing. No one answered. She turned to Jeff, "They're not home yet."

Jeff said, "Do you think they'll move back to Atlanta?"

"I think I would."

"But that's chickening out."

"Look what they're up against, Jeff."

"Do you think anyone would actually attack the Jacksons?"

Crista sat back down and sipped her Coke. Rontu walked over and sat by the table, putting his head in Crista's lap. When she peered down into his crystal-blue eyes, he whimpered and licked her hand. "Even Rontu seems to know something is wrong."

"Dogs sense things. They're much smarter than cats. My grandmother has two cats so I should know."

"We have to do something," Crista said.

"But what?"

"Find out who's doing this."

"How?"

"I don't know how. Be investigators. No one seems to have any idea who could be doing it."

The phone rang, and Crista answered it. It was the woman at the police station who Crista had talked to several days ago. "We checked out the license plate you gave us," the woman said.

"Yes?" Crista looked at Jeff with emboldened eyes. "What did you find out?"

"The owner is a long-time resident," the woman replied. "We charged him once two years ago with DWI—driving while intoxicated—and he lost his license for three months. He has no other black marks on his record. He said he had pulled off the road the other day to take a nap. It didn't wash too well with the officer, but it was a fair alibi. He didn't do anything, so I'm afraid there's nothing we can charge him with. He denies being in the woods when you were fishing. He says it must have been another truck."

The lady stopped talking and Crista didn't know what to ask. Finally, she said, "All right. Thank you." She was about to hang up when she said, "Oh, does he have any kids?"

"Wife and four kids. I'm afraid that's all I can tell you."

"What's the name?"

"I'm afraid I can't give that out. He hasn't been charged, and he required that we keep his name confidential."

"I can't get his name?"

"No, I'm sorry. That's not public information."

Suddenly, Crista's heart was beating hard. She realized this could be dangerous. "Did you give him my name?"

"No, we would not reveal that in such a case."

"Thanks."

"If you see any suspicious behavior, please report it right away," the woman continued. "While this person does not have a record, we have discovered that he may be a part of a clandestine organization—a secret group—in the area. Neo-Nazis. They're very vocal against Jews, Blacks, Hispanics, and Orientals. We've had reports of their activities, but we've never actually charged anyone. We can't prove anything at this time, but we think some of these characters may be involved in the incident at the school this afternoon."

"Neo-Nazis?" Crista asked with a frown.

"New Nazis. Followers of Adolph Hitler. We hadn't seen any activity till recently when a Jewish man received threats in the mail. We're investigating, but we believe some of these people have moved into the area."

"That sounds awful."

"It is. Well, I'm sorry, but that's all the news I have. I wish we could report an arrest, but it appears that Mrs. Jackson and her family are going to be harassed a bit. We hope it doesn't get any more serious than this auto defacing."

"Thanks."

Crista hung up. Jeff looked at her with raised eyebrows. "What's going on?"

She told him about the neo-Nazis.

"Skinheads," Jeff said.

"What?"

"In Germany and some other places, I think also in New York City, maybe Chicago. They're called skinheads. They shave their heads, wear Nazi tattoos, stuff like that. I've seen it in the paper."

"But the man in the truck didn't have his head shaved."

Jeff said, "I think it's only the youth who do the skinhead thing. They're thugs, though. They're very tough, very into weapons and guns, and want to overthrow the government."

"Why on earth do we put up with such people?"

"Because we're a free country. We have to."

"We don't have to," Crista argued. "We just do."

"Sure we have to," Jeff said. "If we don't allow the skinheads, then other groups would be banned. Maybe religious groups or something. Ones that you support. So in order to allow one, we have to allow all."

"Where did you come up with this stuff?" Crista stared at Jeff, astonished. He wasn't usually too smart about such things.

"My grandfather," Jeff admitted. "You know, he's always talking about freedom. He really grinds it into me. He says it all comes from the Bill of

Rights. And if the Bill of Rights isn't for all of us, it's for none of us. If we start limiting it to certain groups, then we infringe on all, and we cease to be a democracy. That's what he says, anyway."

"I guess it makes sense."

"It's only when one group goes too far—like murdering people or something—that the government shuts them down. Like the Ku Klux Klan."

"Yeah, I've heard of that."

"They're still allowed, though," Jeff continued. "And the John Birch Society, and the neo-Nazis. But if they get into violence or anything, they can be convicted. Still, it's on an individual basis. I mean, we even allow communists."

"Communism is practically dead," Crista pointed out.

"Yeah, but when it wasn't, people could be communists, and the U.S. didn't put them away."

"I guess. But what's all this have to do with Kayzee and her family?" Crista fidgeted with a pencil. She liked these kinds of discussions with Jeff. He could be very intelligent when he wanted to.

"Well, if these neo-Nazis do anything to the Jacksons, the law comes down on them."

"But what about *before* they do anything?" Crista said. "If we have to wait till they do something, we could all be dead. And then what good is it?"

"Yeah, that's what my grandfather says is a 'flaw' in the system. We can only convict them *after* they've done something, not before. Unless they start making threats. Then you can get them with all kinds of stuff."

"Like what?"

"If they send the threat through the mail, they can go to jail for something. I don't know what. But my grandfather says sending threats through the mail is a big crime, and people get put away for it. That's why most people don't send threats through the mail." Jeff laughed. "Anyway, not most smart people."

"No, they just write their threats in big red letters on someone's car!"

"Yeah, I suppose," Jeff said quietly, shaking his head.

Crista went to the phone again. She dialed Kayzee's number, but there was still no answer. She said to Jeff, "I guess I'd better start getting dinner ready. Do you want to help?"

"No, I'd better get on home." Jeff stood. "Don't sweat this stuff, Crista. It'll work out. Kayzee's family'll be okay."

"I'm just worried something bad has to happen before anyone pays attention to it."

"No, Mr. Burleson is doing something about it, and others will. You'll see."

"All right. See you tomorrow."

"Yeah." Jeff pulled on his coat, grabbed his backpack, and went out the front door.

After he left, Crista stared out the doorway. Rontu and Tigger came and stood by her. She

half-expected to see the strange truck go by and
make threatening gestures. But all was quiet.

Too quiet.

·10·

A Talk with Dad

"Hello," Crista said, answering the insistent ringing of her phone. It was past ten o'clock. She had gone to her room to read before going to sleep. Her father had already gone to bed.

"It's Kayzee," the girl's voice whispered.

"What's up?" Crista asked.

"They beat up Jamal."

Crista gasped. "What do you mean?"

"He was in a fight today at school. He has a split lip and his eye is bruised. He has some bruises on his arms and back. They really worked him over."

"What's your mom going to do?"

"We were at the hospital all afternoon. He had to have X-rays."

"But what's she going to do?" Crista asked again.

"The boys involved are all on probation now. But with the firecracker thing, they're mostly blaming Jamal. They're saying he's a troublemaker, and they've suspended him for a couple of days. A 'cool off' period. I think it stinks."

Crista took a deep breath. "Do you think your

mom will want to go back to Atlanta?"

Kayzee sighed. "It's up to my dad. She has a call into him now. But he's on a sub. It could be awhile before he has a chance to call back."

"Please don't go, Zee."

"It's not up to me, Crista."

"I know. But I feel like we're good friends now, and I don't want to see you leave."

"I appreciate that."

"Well, tell Jamal I'm sorry about what happened. I'll see you tomorrow morning."

"Good."

At school the next morning, there was an assembly in the cafeteria. Mr. Burleson called together all the teachers and staff and had them on stage. The kids sat at the lunch tables. Two police officers also stood on stage.

Mr. Burleson started the assembly standing at the microphone. "As you all know, there was a rather grave disturbance here yesterday. Someone painted a very nasty slogan on Mrs. Jackson's car. This kind of behavior is not acceptable in our school, in our state, in our country. I hope you all realize the gravity of this circumstance." Mr. Burleson paused and let his words sink in. "This is racism in its worst form. Do you all understand what racism is? In a word, it's denying a person his or her rights because of their race. It's rejecting and hating and making fun of people because they have a different color skin. That is not right. We have laws protecting people from racism, and if there are students in this school who are practicing racism in any form, they will face me and the laws of the state of Pennsylvania."

There was dead silence in the room. No one even coughed.

"We are now looking into what happened yesterday. If any of you have any information or know anything about the people who did this act, I want you to come to me. Anything you share will be confidential. That means you will be kept out of public notice. No one will know who reported anything. These two police officers are here to conduct a full investigation of the incident. If any of you know anything about what happened, do not hesitate to talk to either of these officers. They will keep whatever you tell them confidential."

Mr. Burleson looked out over the crowd. It seemed that his eyes stopped on every face and made a connection. Some kids hung their heads. Others just stared vacantly ahead. Some smiled as they met Mr. Burleson's eyes. A few reflected the same indignation that Mr. Burleson felt.

He said, "Are there any questions?"

No one moved.

Then a little girl's hand went up. She was in second grade. "I like Lukie," she said. "He's nice."

Someone else from the second-grade class stood up. "We don't want Lukie to leave. Or Mrs. Jackson."

Suddenly, Jeff was on his feet. "I think whoever did this should be ashamed of themselves."

A number of kids cheered. But then there was quiet as Mr. Burleson raised his hands. "All right," he said. "Then let's get to work. Let's make the Jackson family feel accepted and wanted, and let's get to the bottom of this problem and fix it."

After getting back to their classroom, most kids cheered for Kayzee and Mrs. Jackson, but Crista noticed Tonya Murphy, Danny Kluziewski, and several others looking grim and angry. She wished she could have placed one of them at Mrs. Jackson's car the day before. But they had all been in class all day. None of them could have done the painting.

On the way home that afternoon, Kayzee and Crista talked excitedly about all that had happened. Kayzee said, "I feel more welcome now than I ever did. It's really a miracle."

"Now if we can only catch the people who did the painting."

"Oh, don't worry about it," Kayzee said. "Mom's car is fixed, and whoever did it is probably totally ashamed of themselves after what happened today."

Crista didn't think so, but she kept quiet. She was glad Kayzee felt so much better.

That night Crista told her dad about all that had happened at school. He said he'd heard about some of it on the news.

"It was on the news?" Crista exclaimed.

"On the radio." Her father grinned. "Don't

worry, you didn't make the headline news on CNN. But it was on the radio."

"Mr. Burleson's speech?"

"No, just a few lines about what was happening. This is big news, I'm afraid."

"I wonder how the Jacksons will feel about that."

"I'm sure they'll be fine." Her father sat down in the easy chair and pulled up a magazine. "I want you to know, though, Crista, I'm proud of you. You've shown a lot of maturity about this. The same way you did with Sarah over vacation time."

"Thanks, Daddy. I'm really happy to be Kayzee's friend."

Dr. Mayfield pressed the rear of the chair back and the footrest came up. He leaned back. Crista said to him, "Daddy, why do you think people hate black people so much? I mean I don't. But obviously some people do."

"I think prejudice is part of fallen human nature," Dr. Mayfield said, looking directly at Crista. "People are proud. They're always looking for some way to make themselves look better than others, feel more important than others, any way they can to exalt themselves over the next guy. We make comparisons. If we're smarter than the next guy, we feel better about ourselves. If we're richer, if we have a nicer house, a better car, we feel more important. It's the same thing with race. People start myths about people of other races. You know, there have always been those who claim that black people are genetically inferior to white people, and so on and so forth. It's all garbage, but people do it. It's a way to make us white folks feel higher up on the ladder than others. If black people are all stupid, or poor, or immoral, or whatever, then we're smart, and good, and decent, and better. So I think it all goes back to pride."

"But some people hate, really hate others. I've seen it on TV. That's not just pride, that's...that's... sin. Just sin."

"That's right, honey. It all comes back to sin." Dr. Mayfield picked up a magazine, but then he looked again at Crista. "Revenge. Hate. Pride. It's all those things. And more. For every prejudiced person, there's probably a different reason he's prejudiced. One had a bad experience with a black person when he was a kid. Another was robbed by a black thug. Another grew up in a family where black people were the enemy. Another person...well, like you say, it all goes back to sin."

"Why is there sin in the world, Daddy?"

Her father laughed. "Good grief, Crista, that's not an easy question." He cleared his throat. Then he said, "You're serious."

"Well, I know something about it, but not much."

"I suppose it all goes back to the beginning, in the Garden of Eden. Or actually, even before that, with the fall of Lucifer, who became Satan. You've learned all that in church."

"Yeah, but I like it when you explain it to me."

He laughed again, a musical, friendly, happy laugh. She always liked it when her father smiled and laughed.

"Lucifer didn't like what God had given him. He became proud. That's generally the way we think of it. We don't know a lot about it. The only places in the Bible that talk about it are in Isaiah 14, I think, and Ezekiel 28. But the point is that Lucifer wanted more, even though God had given him the highest place in creation. He was the leader. He was the number-one created being. No one was above him. He was a cherubim, I think, one of the creatures who ruled over all the other angels and created beings. And he wasn't satisfied. We don't know why. But he just felt God had rooked him, I guess. So he rebelled. He led a third of all the angelic host with him. They decided to start a war with God. Eventually, God created earth and the first people, and Satan tempted them and led them into sin. He did it to ruin what God had started. And so we find ourselves here. He tempts people to rebel against God's laws every day. What's God's first law?"

Crista thought. "To love God with all your heart, soul, mind, and might."

"Right. And what's the second one like it?"

"To love your neighbor as yourself."

"Right. So Satan gets people to hate one another, steal from one another, kill one another, and write nasty words on people's cars, just to make it hard on

God. It's all Satan's way of getting back at God."

Crista was quiet for a moment then shook her head. "Oh well. I guess it all makes sense to God."

Dr. Mayfield laughed. "I'm sure it does, honey. And one day it'll all make sense to us too. Completely."

Crista went back to the kitchen and started dinner. Her mind was full of thoughts about prejudice and Satan and the war going on in the world around her. It was kind of exciting, she thought, to be right in the middle of it.

·11·

Another Truck

Crista peered at the clock. One in the morning. She couldn't sleep. Her mind was filled with the images that she and her father had talked about earlier.

Sitting up, she yawned. She glanced at the easel to the left of her bed. On it were several pictures Mrs. Jackson had given her to do a family portrait. Crista had wanted to get them together live, but Mrs. Jackson said she was very busy. They would try the pictures first.

Crista walked over and flicked on the light at the top of the easel. She had drawn Mr. and Mrs. Jackson sitting in the middle, Lukie to their left, Kayzee on the right, and Jamal over them in the back. They were a handsome family.

Scrutinizing the picture, Crista touched the chalk to various places, making the faces clearer. She would be done by that Saturday. It was the kind of work she loved. But she didn't feel like working on it now.

"Maybe I'll just take the dogs for a quick walk,"

she said out loud. "The fresh air will make these strange thoughts go away."

She dressed quickly and walked out to the main room. Rontu looked up from lying in front of the fireplace. The fire had turned to little more than embers. Only a few coals shone in the dark. Crista patted her hip. "Come here, boy," she whispered. "Want to go for a walk?"

Rontu jumped up and immediately Tigger stirred next to him. Both dogs wagged their tails happily. Crista went back and listened at her father's room. He was snoring lightly. Asleep. "Good," she mumbled. "He won't mind."

She stepped out into the night. Crickets chirruped, making their strange, sawing noise. She heard something rustle over in the leaves and decided it was a nocturnal squirrel. He couldn't sleep either, she thought.

The two dogs and Crista walked out to the dirt road in front of her house. Pimpled with imbedded pebbles and stones, the road was sprayed with an oil residue to keep down the dust. Crista let her sneakers slide on the slightly slick surface for a moment. She stood in the middle of the road. "Which way, guys?" she asked. "To Jeff's or Kayzee's?"

Both dogs just wagged their tails, looking up into Crista's eyes with love. "It's so nice to have real admirers," she said with a chuckle. "All right, to Kayzee's. We'll just take a little walk. Don't get out ahead of me."

A walking stick leaned against a tree at the edge of the little parking area in front of her house. Crista picked it up and tapped it on the ground. "I feel like Moses," she said. She touched each of the dogs' heads with the walking stick. "I dub thee Sir Lancelot and his mighty tyke, Arthur, Junior." She was in a good mood. She knew she'd have to take a long walk now to get sleepy, but she didn't mind. She liked the night, liked the sounds of insects and other creatures, liked the feeling of sliding along in the darkness, seeing but unseen.

She took the first steps toward Kayzee's road. She'd have to cut through the trees, and she didn't like the idea. Who knew what was lurking out there? No, she decided, she'd walk up to the highway, hike down on the gravel shoulder of the road, and catch Kayzee's street where it joined the highway. No reason to go walking through a strange patch of woods at this hour.

She came to the curve up to the main road. Stopping and listening for a moment, the sounds of both dogs panting filled her ears. "You guys sound like you've been hiking for miles," Crista said with a snort. "You must be outta shape bad, real bad."

She chuckled again and clicked the tip of the walking stick on the ground. It made a little *tump tump* noise as it touched the hard-packed road. She held it in her right hand. It was a nice stick. Her dad had stripped it of bark so that it was a brusk white, and he'd also carved a little bearded head at the top.

He was good with his hands that way. Carving was one art Crista had never attempted.

The dogs pattered along, sniffing here and there, darting into the high weeds that grew on the edge of the woods between the houses. Once Rontu barked, a stiff, hard *woof*. But other than that, the night was quiet. Every now and then a big tractor trailer swooshed by on the highway. It seemed they were always on the road at night, gliding along through the darkness with their huge cargoes.

There were no bugs in the air. It was still too early. The weather remained crisp and cool. Crista shivered a few times as they walked along.

They reached the highway and turned right at the mailboxes where she met the school bus each day. On the other side of the road, a truck rattled by, throwing up dust and bits of stone behind it. Crista closed her eyes and covered her mouth and nose. She didn't want to breathe in the smoke that hung in the air behind the truck. Why did they always have to belch such sick black smoke into the air anyway? If someone wanted to do something about the pollution, the first thing was to get rid of smoke-chugging trucks. That would clear up half of it! Crista thought.

The dogs turned instinctively down Midway Drive when they reached it. Crista continued to tap the walking stick on the road in front of her. Somehow carrying a walking stick always gave her a feeling of great security. The cool night with its stars sprayed out above her made her feel quiet inside. Her thoughts felt bottled up, but not tight; just held in place. As if God were speaking peace to her heart.

It was a feeling she liked. She wondered briefly what people who did not know the Lord thought about when things were tough or circumstances in their lives went haywire. Did they have anyone to turn to? Certainly, they could talk to friends and relatives. But there was something different about talking to God, Crista thought. He knew your deepest thoughts. You didn't even have to express how you felt in words, if you couldn't. He understood them before you even felt them. She was glad that God cared for and loved her and her family. But there were so many people in the world who did not know God, and did not care to. How did they survive? How did they cope when things went wrong? Who did they talk to when they didn't even know all the thoughts that churned around inside them?

Crista wondered for a moment if Kayzee and her mom and dad and brothers were Christians. They had gone to her church, so maybe they were. But why didn't she and Kayzee talk about it? It would be the most natural thing in the world to do. She resolved next time she had a chance, she'd ask Kayzee about it.

Crista knew there were some things that every Christian believed in—like that Jesus was God in human flesh, or that the Bible was God's Word, or that Jesus rose from the dead. But she also knew there were other things that Christians could disagree about, things that didn't have to do with being saved or who God is. What were those things? Oh, like whether Christians could dance or play cards or go to movies. Things like that. Crista and her parents had had many discussions about Christianity when her mom was alive. Her mom was always talking about theology.

Her dad, though, didn't talk that much after Crista's mom died. She didn't know why. Maybe he'd always been a quiet person and her mother had made him talk more. Maybe that was what Crista had to do.

She swished along, noticing the little *wish-wish* that her pants made as her legs rubbed together. She looked up at the stars. Soon, she turned at the bottom of the road down to the main houses. Kayzee's house was up about a hundred yards. She knew she wouldn't knock or try to wake anyone up. But she wondered if Kayzee or anyone in her family was lying in bed now, struggling with the same kind of thoughts Crista had been.

Staying to the side of the road, she told the two dogs to keep close. "We're going to go back in a few minutes now, so don't run off," she said. As if they really understood anything she said. She rolled her eyes at the thought.

A moment later, she saw two headlights turn at

the far end of the road. Crista stopped and stepped sideways behind a tree. Who was out driving at this hour?

She watched as the vehicle rattled toward her. Then suddenly its lights went out as it jangled down the road. A second later, it stopped and turned into a driveway. Kayzee's driveway.

Crista dropped her mouth. Was it that strange truck?

No, it was a white, new truck. She could see that under the street lamps.

Keeping close to the trees, she jogged along, trying to get a closer look. She saw the rear lights on the truck go out as the driver let up on the brakes. The car door opened with a searing creak. It was obvious, though, that the person in the truck was trying to be quiet.

Crista crouched in the trees. Her heart was hammering. Who was it?

She grabbed Rontu at the collar and held him. Tigger sat down next to them and scratched himself with his rear foot.

The person stood next to the truck. Between the street lamp light and the light inside the truck cab, Crista could finally see his face.

It was Jamal.

She gasped, then covered her mouth. What was Jamal doing out? And in a truck? Where had the truck come from? Had he been unable to sleep and gone for a drive?

Crista waited in the trees, not moving. Jamal stopped, listened, looked around, then turned and quietly shut the door to the truck. The light inside the cab went out, and his face was shrouded in darkness. He walked up the path to the house, his feet crunching on the ground. Then he silently opened the front door and stepped inside. A moment later, he closed it. No lights went on in the house.

Crista slowly stood. "Come on, guys," she said. "We'd better go. I hope Jamal isn't getting into more trouble."

Both dogs stood and wagged their tails slowly back and forth. Crista hurried back up the road, barely touching the walking stick to the ground.

What was Jamal doing at one in the morning? The fact that he'd been quiet and had turned out the truck lights at the end of the street indicated he didn't want anyone to know he'd been out.

So what was he doing?

"Oh, Lord, I hope it isn't more firecrackers or anything like that," Crista prayed as she jogged down the road.

·12·
A Suspect

"Hey," Crista said to Kayzee as soon as she showed up at the bus stop, "does your mother have a new truck?"

"Oh, it's my dad's," Kayzee said. "A friend of ours had it, and he drove it up yesterday."

"Did you know..." Crista started to say, but she stopped herself. Kayzee was looking at her.

"Did you know what?" Kayzee asked.

"Yeah, what, Crista?" Jeff put in when Crista didn't reply.

"Did you know that Mr. Rader is doing another race today?" Crista said, quickly recovering. She wasn't sure what Kayzee would say if she knew Crista had been out watching their house the night before. Kayzee might think she had been spying on them.

"Of course." Kayzee smiled. "And I'm going to win."

"Not if I have anything to say about it," Jeff huffed, joking. "It's about time we had a new grand master of running."

"No one's going to beat me," Kayzee said confidently.

"You'd better watch out for Danny, though," Crista said. "He's raring to win again."

"I can take him," Kayzee replied cockily. Crista was surprised at how different Kayzee was now from when she'd first arrived. Shy and quiet at first, now she was bold and sure. Things had simmered down since the assembly, and maybe the racism problem was really going to go away.

The bus pulled up to the stop and the kids boarded. Crista took a seat in the front, with Kayzee next to her and Jeff across the aisle. Crista mulled over the question that was burning in her mind. Finally she found a way to ask it.

"Jamal is sixteen, right?"

"Yeah," Kayzee answered, watching the trees as the bus passed down the road toward Danny Kluziewski's stop.

"I guess he has his driver's license."

"Yeah, just got it recently," Kayzee said absently. "He didn't have one in Georgia, but up here I guess it's easier to get one."

"So he could drive your mom's car?"

"Or the truck." Suddenly, Kayzee looked at her quizzically. "Why all the questions?"

"Just wondering." Crista tried to sound casual. "I thought I saw Jamal driving yesterday, and I was surprised."

"Oh, he's always out in Dad's truck now. Thinks

he's gonna take it over while Dad's gone. Calls it his machine." She laughed.

Crista breathed with some relief, although she still hadn't gotten to the main issue about Jamal being out in the middle of the night. There was no way at this point she was going to ask about that.

After getting to class, Kayzee sat at her desk next to Crista. When she opened it, she gasped.

Crista looked across at her friend. "What is it?" she whispered, as Mrs. Roberts called for attention.

Kayzee pointed. On top of the pile of books in her desk was a Mars Bar, and beneath it was an envelope.

"What is it, Zee?" Crista asked, keeping her voice low.

"I don't know. There was one here yesterday and..."

Mrs. Roberts called for attention. "Girls, quiet now. I don't want any more talking."

"At recess," Kayzee mouthed.

Two hours later at recess, Kayzee showed it all to Crista. "There was a note like this yesterday. I'll show it to you." She took out her purse. "And another candy bar. Look, the note says, 'Hang in there. Things will get better. Guaranteed.'"

She opened up the note from the day before. Crista read it: "There are people watching who want you to succeed." That was all.

Crista was astonished. "Who do you think is doing it?"

"Someone in the class," Kayzee said. "Do you think?"

"Someone who cares," Crista said. "I think it's great."

"So do I. I especially like the candy bar." She pulled it out of her purse. "Want a piece?"

"Sure."

The girls ate until Mr. Rader called them over for the race.

Kayzee won the race, and Danny Kluziewski walked about ranting and raving that he had been tripped, but no one backed that up. Kayzee had been separated from him by two other runners.

Of course, Jeff didn't even run in the finals, as he'd jokingly vowed. But he performed some antics at the finish line that had everyone laughing. He raced around, grinning and eeping like a monkey. Mr. Rader had to calm everyone down with a stiff reprimand to Jeff to take things seriously. Danny was especially angry, because Jeff bounded up to him after the race, still acting like a monkey, and cheeped, "You number two. You number two."

That afternoon, after walking Kayzee home, Crista saw Jamal riding around in the truck alone. She noticed a large toolbox stretched across the truck bed behind the cab, easily big enough to fit into. For a moment, a plan flashed into her mind, but she wasn't sure she could pull it off. She said to Jeff, "How would you like to do a little investigating with me?"

"What?" Jeff asked.

"I'm not sure yet, but it might be dangerous. Think you could do it?"

"Tell me what it is and I'll let you know."

"I'll tell you tomorrow. If something happens tonight."

"What?" Jeff swaggered along, took out his slingshot, and shot a pebble into some tree branches.

"I'll have to see. I'll let you know." She liked being mysterious with Jeff sometimes. It kept him on his toes.

That night, as Crista was preparing dinner, her father walked into the kitchen. "More trouble out on the main highway," he said.

Crista turned from cooking some hamburger with green peppers and onions and looked at him. "What happened?"

"Someone broke into the Dairy Queen out by the elementary school. Took a little cash out of the cash register, and then they trashed the place.

Crista's heart sank. Was that what Jamal was doing?

"When did it happen?" Crista asked, afraid to hear the answer.

"Last night."

Crista felt like she wanted to throw up. "Who do they think did it?"

"They don't know."

Crista turned back to the steaming meat. Her

father shrugged. "I just wondered..."

"You mean, Jamal Jackson?"

"Yeah, I was thinking...you know."

"Daddy, I don't think he would do it." Did she really? "He's already in enough trouble." But some kids got into a lot of trouble. And Jamal had been in plenty of trouble in Atlanta.

She resolved then and there to go out that night and see if Jamal went anywhere.

That evening Crista went to her room after finishing her homework to read and think and pray. Her father finally went to bed at ten o'clock. The next two hours went by at a turtle's pace. Crista felt so nerve-wracked. She didn't want to find out that Jamal was the culprit, but something within her drove her to investigate. Maybe it was her natural desire that people be treated fairly. She wanted to prove Jamal was innocent—first to herself, and then to anyone else who asked. No way Jamal had robbed the Dairy Queen. There was just no way.

·13·
What She Saw

After pulling on her coat at midnight, Crista slipped out of the house. The dogs didn't come this time. She decided she didn't want them to make a noise that would betray her presence. The air was cold, and a quarter moon lit up the sky. The night was filled with stars. It was glorious, but she was troubled by what she was doing. What if she found out that Jamal had been robbing stores? What would she do then?

She flicked on her flashlight to make sure it was working. Then she flicked it off. She could see well enough by the starlight. The occasional street lamps that stood about a hundred yards apart on the sides of the road illuminated the area enough to see a person's face or anything else.

Her heart pounded in her chest. Why was she even doing this? What if Jamal saw her and turned vicious? She hadn't thought about that. Now the thought surprised and alarmed her. Maybe this wasn't such a good idea after all.

No, she told herself, she had to find out. Too

many things were happening too fast. It seemed more likely that someone might be trying to set up someone like Jamal, just for spite, or hatred. Fortunately, Kayzee hadn't mentioned any questioning by the police. Wouldn't they normally come out and question prospective suspects? If they thought Jamal might be doing this, wouldn't they investigate?

Her heart seemed to stop for a moment, then beat loudly again. All right, there was no reason to panic. Maybe it was just a coincidence. Surely Jamal wasn't that stupid as to get into more trouble already. No, there had to be a more logical explanation.

Nonetheless, the idea troubled her. "What if's" sped through her mind.

She soon reached Midway Drive through the little cut in the trees at the bottom of Rock Road. She stayed close to the trees, being careful not to sway branches or rub against the dry dead leaves still hanging in some places in a way that would make noise.

There was a street lamp near Kayzee's house, shining brightly. Crista could see the truck parked in its spot in the driveway. So Jamal hadn't gone yet. If he was going at all.

Mrs. Jackson's car was also parked in the driveway. All the red paint had fortunately been scoured away where the neo-Nazis or whoever they were had written the terrible slogan. Crista didn't know whether they had repainted the car, or whether they were able to get the paint off with some chemicals. But it was off. That was a relief.

She scurried from hiding spot to hiding spot down the road. Soon she stood in the lot next to the Jacksons' house. The lights were out in the house. No one appeared to be up and about. Crista crouched down in the bushes and watched. She sat back on her haunches, thinking again. She decided to pray, but wasn't sure what to pray. Finally, she just murmured under her breath, "Please, Lord, don't let Jamal be into something bad. I don't think the Jacksons can take it, and I don't think the school can take it, and I don't think I can take it. So please, let it be something else."

Time passed slowly. She kept glancing at her watch. Twelve-oh-seven. Twelve-oh-nine. Twelve-twelve. "Come on," Crista murmured. "If something's going to happen, let it happen."

She heard something. A creak. The front door. Then the screen door opened. It was Jamal.

Crista breathed tightly. All right, he really was doing something. What was the next step? Find out where he was going. And there was only one way.

Waiting and watching, Crista observed Jamal sneak out of the house. Crista noticed there was something in his hand. A package. What was that?

He reached the truck, clambered in, and turned the ignition but he didn't let the engine roar; it only purred. He slipped it into gear and backed out. He didn't turn on the lights.

Crista watched as he drove down the road. At the corner, the lights came on.

He disappeared around the bend. Crista looked at her watch. Twelve-sixteen. Should she wait till he came back? She yawned. She wanted to go to sleep. She'd never be able to get up the next morning. But somehow she had to see when Jamal came back.

She stood and stretched, shook her legs a couple of times, and thought through a couple Scriptures she'd memorized. "Philippians 1:6," she recited in her mind. "I am confident of this very thing that he who began a good work in you will perfect it until the day of Christ Jesus."

Shaking her leg again because it had fallen asleep, she recited several other Scriptures. But she came back to Philippians 1:6. Was it really true that God would see you all the way to the end? That He would "perfect" you right up to the finish? That was what it said. Somehow it comforted her. Knowing that God was always there, always watching over her and making sure the right circumstances combined to get her where she had to go, was a wonderful feeling. It meant she didn't really have to fear anything in this life.

But what about the Jacksons? Did they believe that God would see them through this? She remembered that she still wanted to talk to Kayzee about Jesus. But so far the time never seemed right.

She looked at her watch. Still only twelve-thirty-two. "Come on, Jamal. Come home."

Wishing she wasn't doing this, she waited and waited. It seemed as if time stood still. She thought about all the times she wished that time could just stop, and she could do whatever she wanted while nothing else happened in the whole world. Take a nap. Draw a picture. Not go to school. But right now she wished time would fly. She wanted to be home, safe in her own bed.

Finally, lights appeared on the road. Crista sank down into her crouch. Just at the bend, the lights went off. It was Jamal.

She waited until he'd parked and gone into the house. Then she waited another five minutes. When she was sure he'd gone to bed, she stepped out of the bushes, crept over to the truck, and looked inside. There was a small bag on the seat. She silently opened the truck door and looked in. The bag was empty. What had been in it?

She turned it over. A receipt fluttered out. She looked at the little white slip of paper. Then she grabbed it and stuffed it into her pocket. She closed the door as quietly as she could.

Next she looked into the bed of the truck. The large metal toolbox stood right behind the cab. Was anything in it? Her heart was pounding now. Should she risk getting into the truck and looking into the toolbox?

Yeah, she had to. If she was going to do this investigation, she had to go all the way.

She placed her right foot on the little ledge in

front of the wheel well. She climbed up, threw
her left foot over, and hunched down behind
the toolbox. It had a latch and a place for a lock.
But there was no lock. She opened the latch, then
started to lift the top of the toolbox. Her heart
seemed to be hammering right into her throat. She
kept glancing at the door of the house, but no lights
came on.

She pulled the lid up.

It was empty.

Letting it down, she breathed heavily. She felt
tired and exhilarated at once. At least Jamal wasn't
hiding anything in the toolbox. She closed the lid
and the latch. Then she climbed over the lip of the
bed. She was down on the ground a moment later.

Brushing her hands off, she took one last look
into the cab and then headed down the road. She felt
in her pocket for the receipt. Maybe that would tell
her something.

When she reached Rock Road, she took out the
slip of paper and turned on the flashlight. It was just
a common payment receipt. It read, "MCHDSE"—
that meant "Merchandise," she was sure. Across on
the other side: "$0.50." Then, "TX," for "Tax," and
it read, "$0.03." "TOTAL: $0.53."

What on earth was all that about?

Crista sped home. She had to solve this mystery.
She had to. And soon. But next she needed to con-
vince Jeff to come along.

·14·
The Ride

"Jeff, please," Crista said to her best friend. "I can't do it alone."

"But what if he catches us?" Jeff asked. "If he's doing something bad, we could be in big trouble."

"He's not going to catch us."

"I don't know, Crista. It's risky."

"Look, I'll let you get all the glory if we find out anything. You can have your name in the paper. You can say it was even your idea."

"I don't think I care too much about that."

Crista spotted Kayzee coming up the road. "All right, be quiet about it. I don't want Kayzee to know yet. She already has enough trouble. If her brother's doing something bad, it should be broken to her slowly and gently."

"Yeah, I agree with that." Jeff turned and grinned. "Hi, Zee!"

Kayzee walked up. She took off her large backpack and leaned it against her foot. "So what's up with you two?"

"Nothing much," Crista said, immediately feeling

guilty about not leveling with Kayzee. But she didn't want to go to Kayzee with an accusation that wasn't true. Kayzee didn't need that, and neither did she.

Kayzee looked up the road. "Here comes the bus. Right on time."

"As always," Crista said. She wondered if Kayzee would think she was betraying her. No, Kayzee would understand, she hoped.

When they arrived at the school, there was a commotion going on out front. Everyone had gathered at the main doors, and Mr. Burleson was trying to get the situation under control. Kayzee, Jeff, and Crista ran over as soon as they jumped off the bus.

"What's going on?" Crista said to no one in particular.

"Another painting," someone said.

Then Crista saw it. "N—— die!" It was painted right across the front doors of the school.

Mr. Burleson had a bullhorn now. "Everyone to their classes," he announced. "We'll take care of this!"

Crista put her arm around Kayzee. "Come on. Let's get to class."

Kayzee's face was cloudy with anger. "I hate this place. I hate it!"

Crista glanced at Jeff and said nothing. He simply hung his head. "It's wrong," he muttered. "Who could be doing this?"

No sooner had their class settled down when Mr.

Burleson's voice came over the intercom, asking Kayzee to join her brother Lukie and her mom in his office. After she left, Mrs. Roberts asked everyone to watch out for Kayzee.

"It's not right and it's not fair," Mrs. Roberts said. "We all know who this racism is directed at, and we must gather around her and be strong. The people who are perpetrating this will be caught. Mark my words on that."

Everyone was silent when Kayzee shuffled back into the room, her head hanging. It was plain she'd been crying. When Kayzee sat down, Crista reached across and squeezed her hand, but Kayzee pulled away. Crista decided not to push it. Kayzee needed her space.

At recess, Jeff told Crista, "I'll come with you. I think we need to help the Jacksons all we can. And if Jamal's in trouble, we need to help him."

"I agree," Crista said. She explained her plan.

"That sounds good to me," he agreed.

Kayzee didn't talk much that day and stayed out of everyone's way. She didn't even get any hard looks from Danny Kluziewski. Crista thought about just telling Mrs. Jackson what she'd seen with Jamal. But she really didn't know if it was anything. What if Jamal simply couldn't sleep and was taking a nighttime drive? What harm was there in that? She didn't want to jump the gun, as her father said she did sometimes. And at the same time, she didn't want to give the Jacksons more trouble than they already had.

That night, after Dr. Mayfield had gone to bed, Crista waited for Jeff's signal. When he flashed his light on her windows in the back of the house, she came out.

"Ready?" she asked.

"Loaded for bear," Jeff said, showing her his slingshot.

"What's that for?"

"Bear," Jeff said, chuckling.

They set off down the road. In ten minutes, they stood in the woods outside the Jacksons' house. All was quiet and dark. Crista led Jeff to the side of truck. "I think he comes out about twelve-fifteen, so we have plenty of time." It was just past twelve o'clock.

"It's going to be cramped."

"Yeah, but we'll make it."

Crista silently climbed aboard the truck in the back. She took out some tape.

"What's that for?" Jeff whispered, watching.

"Tape back the latch. We don't need it falling over and locking us in there."

"Good idea."

She taped the latch up against the lid of the large toolbox. Then she opened it. "I'll get in first." She moved inside, lying on her back with her legs crimped up. It wasn't that uncomfortable. She hoped Jamal wouldn't take too long, though.

"All right, I'm coming in," Jeff whispered. Setting his feet by Crista's head, he crammed himself into the box. "It's tight," he said. But he got all the way in.

"Now pull down the lid," Crista said.

Jeff did it. They were both thrust into pitch blackness. Crista snapped on her flashlight, shining it on Jeff's face. He was all squinched up at the other end.

"I feel like a sardine," he said.

"Just wait. In fifteen minutes, you'll feel like a dead sardine, and then an eaten one." She smiled and clicked off the flashlight. "Now we just wait."

Time trudged along, but soon they heard footsteps, then the door opening. The engine started.

"Here we go," Crista whispered. "About to find out the great secret."

"It might not be some great secret, Crista," Jeff said.

"Just be quiet."

They both snuggled down in the box. Every bump knocked against Crista's back, and it hurt. She realized now why they padded seats in trucks. This was painful! Each knock whacked through her like a shot. She was beginning to feel this wasn't such a good idea. The truck clanked down the road, and soon she felt the smoothness and the speed of the highway. The road whooshed under her. The whirring of the wheels rang in her ears. The radio inside the cab crackled on, and Crista could hear Jamal playing rap tunes. Loud.

"I wonder what bands he likes," Crista whispered.

"Not the same ones as me," Jeff replied.

The truck came to a stop.

"The main light on 507," she said.

"Right," Jeff agreed. "Feel which way he goes."

"To the right," Crista said as the truck lurched past the light.

She held her breath. The Dairy Queen and other stores were on the left side of the road. But Jamal didn't stop.

Then she felt the truck turning off to the side. Gravel clicked under the wheels.

"Where are we?" Jeff asked.

"Somewhere close to the turn," Crista answered.

She felt the truck crunch to a stop. The engine died. The door opened, then shut. She heard keys jingling.

Waiting, the darkness plunged in, making Crista feel even tighter than she was. She could barely breathe with all the anxiety building in her.

"We should lift the lid," she finally said.

"Yeah," Jeff agreed. "We have to risk it."

He pushed the lid up slowly. When it was cracked about six inches, he stopped and listened. They heard a door open and shut in the distance. Crista looked out. And gasped.

"It's the school parking lot!" she exclaimed.

"What's he doing here?" Jeff asked.

Crista froze. Could Jamal have been the one who painted the awful sign on the door, and on his own mother's car?

It made her feel sick at heart. Surely Jamal wouldn't do such a thing. Unless...unless he wanted to get them all to go back to Atlanta.

No, he wouldn't!

"Let's take a look," she said, trying to calm the thoughts racing through her head.

Jeff pushed the lid all the way up, being careful not to make a noise. As he stood, Crista pulled herself up. They both kept low behind the cab of the truck, not wanting to stick their heads out and be seen. They stared at the school through the windows of the cab.

"What on earth is he doing here?" Jeff whispered.

"Maybe we should get off the truck and go see."

"But how?"

"I don't know. Look inside the windows. He went inside, didn't he?"

"It looks like it. See—the door there—it's open."

"All right, let's run over to the door and look inside."

"But what if he's coming back and he catches us?"

Crista shook her head. "It's all the way or nothing. We're going to get to the bottom of this."

"All right," Jeff sighed, "let's go."

They both jumped off the truck and hurried to the door. Looking inside, they waited, listening. Suddenly, they heard whistling. It was Jamal.

It was getting closer.

"He's coming! Let's get back," Jeff said.

He and Crista nearly fell over one another rushing back to the truck. They had just climbed aboard when they saw Jamal at the door. He turned around to shut it. Jeff opened the lid to the toolbox, but it was too late. Jamal was already turning around to look at the truck.

"Get down in the back," Jeff mouthed, closing the lid and scrunching up in a ball behind the toolbox. Crista followed, just as Jamal finished locking the door. They heard his sneakers crunching on the blacktop as he came toward them.

Jeff lay up against the side of the truck bed. Crista was on the other side. If Jamal looked inside, he'd see her easily. She slid over next to Jeff and pushed as close as she could.

Jamal walked over to the truck, stopped, listened, then opened the door.

Crista breathed with relief. At least he hadn't seen them. Not yet.

The truck engine purred, and Jamal pitched it into gear. With a jolt, he sped out of the parking lot. The bottom of the truck bed bumped and jumped with each defect in the road. Crista's cheek and temple felt bruised.

The ride back up the mountain seemed like an eternity. When they finally pulled into the Jacksons' driveway, Jamal got out, but he didn't look in the back of the truck where Crista and Jeff lay mashed up against the toolbox. When they heard the door to the house close, they both let out a sigh of relief.

When they were sure Jamal had gone to bed, Crista sat up and looked at the house. It was dark and quiet. The moon shone above them, and the air was crisp and chilly. Crista jumped over the side of the truck and Jeff followed. She looked into the cab again and saw another bag. She opened the truck door and grabbed the bag, but it was empty. This time there was no receipt slip.

She closed the door and turned. "Let's go."

"What's with the bag?"

She explained what had happened the night before.

"Interesting," Jeff said as they hurried down the street.

Crista's jaw felt tight. She blinked her eyes repeatedly, trying to drive out all the thoughts that were streaming through her brain. Had Jamal robbed the school? No, he didn't have anything in his hands except that bag. And it was empty.

Then what was he up to? What could he be doing? Had he written something inside the school? Had he painted some awful words inside one of the classrooms?

Crista shook her head. "I've got to tell Zee," she said. "I can't keep it inside any longer."

"What do you think she'll say?"

"I don't know." Crista frowned. "But I have to let her know."

"Good luck on that one."

·15·
Suspicious!

At the bus stop the next morning, Crista waited for Kayzee to come up the road. When she appeared with Lukie by her side, Crista took a deep breath. Should she speak up now, or wait to see if anything had been done to the school?

When Kayzee reached the bus stop, Crista greeted her warmly. Kayzee just shrugged. "I'm only wondering what terrible thing we'll find when we get to school today."

"Maybe there won't be anything."

Jeff gave Crista a nudge. She knew what it meant. But she felt she had to wait.

The bus rolled down the road toward them. Everyone climbed aboard. Kayzee sat with Lukie this time, behind Crista and Jeff. Lukie chattered on and on about a story he'd learned in class about a bear. Jeff laughed at the exploits of someone called "hairy bear," and Crista got a chuckle, too. Kayzee was surprisingly quiet.

No one discovered any nasty slogans or other disasters that morning when they arrived at school.

Crista continued to wonder what Jamal might have done.

Suddenly, Mr. Burleson came on the loudspeaker. "All students file out to the parking lot immediately. Teachers, guide your students for the fire drill."

Crista, Jeff, and Kayzee filed out with the rest of their classmates. Everyone stood in lines outside the school, nervously whispering to each other, when it was announced that someone had called to say there was a bomb in the school. Police cars arrived with a special "bomb squad" unit.

The kids stood outside, shivering in the morning air, as the day clouded over and a cold front lashed in from the west.

"What if it goes off?" Jeff asked. "That'll be the ultimate."

"I don't think having a bomb go off is the ultimate," Crista said.

Kayzee didn't respond. When Crista asked her what was wrong, she said, "It's because of us again. Someone is doing this, and I know we're going to get hurt. I think we should just go home to Atlanta."

As they stood in line, Crista mulled over what she knew about Jamal. Finally, she decided to mention it to Kayzee. "Jeff and I did something last night I think you need to know about," Crista began.

Kayzee gave Crista her immediate attention. "What did you do?"

"I happened to see something three nights ago that worried me. I got up, couldn't sleep, and took a walk with the dogs. I saw your brother, Jamal, come back in your dad's truck about one o'clock. He turned off the lights when he reached your part of the road and parked the truck quietly. It was like he didn't want anyone in the house to hear. Your house."

"So? Jamal's always going out in that truck now."

"Yeah, but at twelve-fifteen? And turning off the lights so no one will see him? Do you think your mom knows about it?"

"What else did he do? My mom hasn't said anything to me about it."

Crista glanced at Jeff, who raised his eyebrows dramatically and indicated that she should go easy. "That was the night the Dairy Queen was robbed, Kayzee."

Looking at her with dark, angry eyes, Kayzee said, "What happened next?"

"Then the night before last, I got up to see if he did it again. Sure enough, he did. I saw him come out with a little bag. It had this in it." She showed Kayzee the receipt. "That was the night before the day we found that awful writing on the front of the school."

Kayzee took the receipt, looked at it, and glared at Crista. "You think Jamal would do that?" Kayzee folded her arms.

"I don't know," Crista said. "I don't know. I'm

just telling you this because I'm worried. What if something bad is going on?"

"So what did you do last night?"

Crista took a deep breath. This was the biggie. "Last night, Jeff and I hid in the toolbox on the back of the truck to see where Jamal was going. He drove down the hill and came here, to the school. And now we have a bomb scare."

Kayzee's mouth dropped open. "You think Jamal did all this stuff?"

Crista swallowed hard. "I don't know. I'm not saying that. It's just that we don't know what he was doing each of those nights. And now every day so far that he did it, something awful has happened."

"And you think Jamal did all of those things?" Kayzee's eyes were steady and unrelenting. She didn't flinch. She didn't blink. She stared right into Crista's eyes. Crista could feel the anger in them, and it made her afraid.

"So you were spying on my brother?"

"Not spying," Crista said quickly. "Just trying to find out what was going on."

Kayzee glanced from Crista to Jeff and back. "I thought you were my friends. But you're just like all white people. Suspicious. Never giving black people a chance. Coming down on them. Spying."

"Kayzee, that's not what I meant..."

"Then what did you mean?"

"I'm concerned. I want to help. I want to get to the bottom of this. I want to find out who or what or why these people are..."

"And you think my brother wrote that word on the wall? You think he would write that about his own people?"

"No. But..."

"And you think he robbed the Dairy Queen, too? You think he just drove down there and broke in and stole the money and that's what he's all about? Thieving and stealing and hurting people?"

"No, Kayzee, no. I don't know."

Several kids were staring at the two girls now. Everyone stood openmouthed as Kayzee went on.

"And now you think my brother planted a bomb in our school?"

"I don't know, Kayzee! I'm not the police!"

"You sure act like it!" Kayzee turned around. She walked forward to the front of the line and spoke with Mrs. Roberts. A moment later, Mrs. Roberts looked up and walked back to Crista.

"What is going on here, Crista?" Mrs. Roberts asked. "Kayzee says you've accused her brother of all kinds of terrible things."

"No, Mrs. Roberts. It's all a mistake. Kayzee, I'm sorry, I didn't mean..."

"Some friend you are!" Kayzee said. She turned and stalked off. A minute later, Crista saw her talking with her mother over by one of the other classes.

Jeff said to Crista, "I think you came on a little strong there, Crista. I..."

"Why don't you just be quiet?"

"Hey, don't get mad at me now. You're the one who had to do this. I just came along for the ride."

Crista turned to the side, folding her arms. Tears burned in her eyes. What was she going to do? How could she make this right?

Mr. Burleson came on the loudspeaker as kids waited restlessly in the parking lot. Police appeared at the front doors, walked through, and went to their cruisers.

"Teachers and students," Mr. Burleson was saying, "the police have not found anything to indicate a bomb in the building. We believe this was a prank call. Please go to your classrooms and take your seats quietly."

The kids filed in slowly. No one said much, and Kayzee remained with her mother until she was inside the building. Then she slipped into the classroom and took her seat, saying nothing.

Crista felt upset and confused. What had she done wrong? She wanted to make it right, but she didn't know how.

Mrs. Roberts stood in front of the classroom. "It appears that the person or persons involved with this bomb scare are determined to promote their racism. We are not going to tolerate these actions. This is very serious, kids. Calling up and saying a bomb is in the school is a major offense. Furthermore, if you know anything that might lead to the capture of this person, please raise your hand or come to me after class. Anything you say will remain confidential."

Kayzee glanced at Crista. Crista, for her part, was not going to say anything about Jamal. But it troubled her. She didn't want to become Kayzee's enemy, but it looked like that was exactly what had happened.

At recess that afternoon, Kayzee kept to herself, playing mostly on the playground equipment with the other kids. She didn't speak with Crista at all.

Crista played kickball with Jeff and about ten other kids. She kept looking over at Kayzee and praying that a way would be made for them to reconcile. She thought of apologizing, but she still didn't know what Jamal was doing. Why would he write words on the school that were hateful to all black people? And why would he do things like a bomb scare that could land him in big trouble? It didn't make any sense. She had to find a way to get Kayzee to go with her tonight and find out the truth once for all.

On the bus that afternoon, Kayzee didn't appear. Crista thought she might be going home with her mother. Lukie was missing, too.

On the walk home, Jeff didn't offer much solace. He suggested they go horseback riding, but Crista didn't want to do that. She wanted to be alone, to think and to pray.

·16·
Jeff's Mission

At her house, Crista stood in front of the easel. She was just about done with the Jacksons' portrait. Kayzee hadn't asked her about it in several days. Maybe with recent events, she'd even forgotten about it.

Suddenly, Crista decided she wanted to finish the portrait and get it down to the Jackson house. Maybe that would patch things up.

She sat down and began the fine strokes to finish Mrs. Jackson's face. As her eyes moved back and forth between the portrait and the picture, she caught all the little flourishes of light and shadow that made someone's face unique and singular. She found just the right oval for Mrs. Jackson's almond-shaped eyes. Her slightly turned-up nose was captured in several deft strokes. Soon she had a nearly exact likeness.

She moved on to Mr. Jackson, whom she'd never met. He was a handsome man, with short brushed-back hair, a touch of gray here and there, and a flat, broad nose. His strong brows shadowed striking, almost fiercesome, dark eyes that had just the right touch of humility and care to make him appear tough yet tender.

Crista drew in the last few strokes to finish Mr. Jackson's face. Finally, she turned to Jamal. She'd been avoiding finishing him. Her heart just wasn't in it. And something was blocking her now. She kept trying to get the angle on his chin and jaw, but it always came out wrong. And that was messing up the picture.

But she had to finish it—*today*. She had to get things right with Kayzee.

She worked on Jamal for another half hour. Soon she thought she had his look down, but he definitely wasn't done as well as the others in the family.

Well, it would have to do, Crista thought. She didn't have time to work on the portrait all night.

She sprayed the paper with the charcoal-setting solution so that it would not smudge. Then she rolled it up and tied a red bow around it.

Heading down the street with Rontu and Tigger at either side, she whistled for the first time that day. Rontu's ears twitched and he wagged his tail. Tigger just pranced to her right, looking for all the world like a winner of a dog show.

She stepped through the woods at the end of Rock Road and strolled out to Midway Drive. It was then she saw Jeff. He walked toward her, swaggering and strutting along like he'd just won an award, too. He and Tigger would have made a great pair.

Jeff marched over to Crista. "It's all taken care of," he said.

"What's taken care of?"

"You and Kayzee."

Crista stared at him, perplexed. "What do you mean?"

"I fixed it."

"How?"

"I told her you have...you have...well, a malady known as schizo-myestemia lullalase and..."

"A what?"

"A mental illness."

Crista's eyes flashed with anger. "What do you mean? You told Kayzee that I'm mentally ill?"

"In so many words."

"Jeff!"

"Crista, don't worry about it. Now she feels sorry for you. She's willing to make it all up, if you'll only commit yourself to the institution in Scranton."

"What?"

"All you have to do is sign on the dotted line."

"Jeff!"

Jeff grinned. "No, I didn't tell her you were mentally ill."

"Then what did you do?"

Jeff suddenly turned around. There Kayzee stood in the road. She was dressed for a walk, and she was walking toward them.

"Why don't I let her tell you."

Kayzee joined them, smiling. "Hi, Crista. I didn't expect to meet you here."

"Neither did I," Crista said. "What did Jeff tell you?"

"About Thunder."

Crista looked at Jeff. "What about Thunder?"

"How he had gone through the ice," Kayzee continued, "and you helped Jeff rescue him with Mr. Wilkins."

"But what does that have to do with..." Crista paused, "with us?"

"He told me about what had gone before."

Kayzee glanced at Jeff. "He told me how you followed him one night when he was tracking the cabin wreckers. And how he felt betrayed. He said he had been accused by one of the ladies on your street of being one of the cabin wreckers. And you weren't sure he really wasn't one of them. But then you helped him prove the truth. And not only did you help him rescue the horse, but you got him off the hook."

"But what does that have to do with...?" Crista stammered, not knowing what to say.

"He said you're the most loyal person he ever knew." Kayzee looked at Jeff, her eyes shining. "And he said you would never do anything to hurt me. You're in the business of helping, not hurting."

Crista looked at Jeff, tears brimming in her eyes. "You told her that?"

Jeff hung his head and shrugged. "Sort of. I think

she saw more in it than I did."

"I'm sorry for doubting you," Kayzee said. "I know you are my friend, my friend no matter what. And I shouldn't have said all those things about white people. It's just that sometimes black people have a hard time trusting you. And it just got out of control today."

"I'm so sorry," Crista said. She held out her arms and suddenly both girls embraced. They were crying now, and Jeff stood by, not knowing what to say.

Letting go, Crista and Kayzee stood back, smiling and wiping away tears.

"I finished the drawing." Crista held out the rolled paper.

"Oh, let's see!" Kayzee said, clapping her hands.

Crista handed the drawing with the red ribbon around it to Kayzee. She pulled off the ribbon and unrolled the paper. When she had it open all the way, she gasped.

"It's beautiful!" Kayzee exclaimed. "It's wonderful. My mom will love it."

"I hope so," Crista said.

Everyone stood there not knowing what to say for a moment. Then Crista said, "About Jamal, I don't think..."

"That's all worked out, too," Kayzee interrupted, her voice suddenly low. "Jamal has messed things up pretty bad. And if he's doing something, I guess my mom deserves to know about it. So tonight, we're going to find out what's going on."

"But how?"

"You and me will go in the truck, just like you and Jeff did last night. We'll find out what's going on and, hopefully, we'll find out my brother isn't doing anything wrong. I'm tired of sitting around waiting for the next bad thing to happen. This time we're going to get ahead of it."

Crista smiled. "You really want to?"

"Yes," Kayzee said. "Now I'm curious. And when I get curious, nothing stands in my way!"

Jeff chuckled.

"Come on," Kayzee said, "let's go show my mom. She'll love it."

The three of them hurried back to Kayzee's house. In a few minutes, Mrs. Jackson was marveling at the picture and thanking Crista for such a fine job. But when Jamal walked into the room, there was a sudden silence.

"Don't look like me," Jamal said, after taking a quick glance at the picture. "But everyone else is okay."

Crista swallowed. She had not seen Jamal up close. Something about him looked hard.

She prayed in her mind, "Lord, help us find out what this is all about. And I pray no one is doing anything wrong."

·17·

Down the Mountain

Crista and Kayzee sat hunched over in the toolbox on Mr. Jackson's truck. Crista felt sure Jamal had no idea they were there. She prayed again that they would find out that Jamal wasn't doing anything wrong. But what if he was? Crista refused to think about that.

As Jamal drove along, Crista cracked open the lid of the box. Behind them she saw two lights—a car or a truck—but she didn't worry about it. Even at twelve-thirty, there were usually cars on the road. She watched as the highway zipped along. It was always a strange feeling to watch things from the back rather than the front. It was a sort of whooshy, gutsy feeling that always made her feel like she was flying.

"Do you think Jeff forgot?" Kayzee asked quietly. Jeff had planned to meet them before they got into the truck and to stand guard at the Jackson house until they got back. But he hadn't shown up.

"Maybe he couldn't get out for some reason." Crista frowned. She hoped there was no trouble because now they didn't have Jeff for backup.

"Do you think Jamal is going to the school?" Kayzee said as Crista let the lid of the toolbox back down. In the dark, the air was warm from the heat of their bodies. The closed-in space felt tight and black. Crista couldn't see Kayzee's face except when she opened the lid a little.

"So far it looks like it," Crista said. "Do you think he did the bomb scare?"

Kayzee sighed. "I don't know, Crista. I don't know what my brother could be doing. Unless..."

"Unless what?"

"No, it's just too farfetched. I'll tell you later."

"Okay."

They rode along in silence. The tires of the truck whirred underneath them. Every time there was a slowing down, speeding up, or stop, Crista felt the pressure against the sides of the box. Her back began to ache. She wished Jamal would hurry up and get where he was going. Then the vehicle came to a stop.

"Must be the main road," she said to Kayzee.

"Yeah, I think so."

"Feel which way it's turning."

Crista felt the pitch of the truck to the right. The inertia pushed her back against the rear of the toolbox and also toward Kayzee.

"He's going the right way to get to school," Kayzee said.

"Yeah. It's only a short ride from here." She pushed up the lid and looked out. Now there were two vehicles behind her. She couldn't see what they were, but their headlamps remained fixed on the back of the truck. She let down the lid right away. She didn't want them seeing her, whoever they were—even if they were just passing through.

Crista felt the truck turning again. Yes, Jamal was going to the school.

Moments later, the truck crunched to a stop on the asphalt. Jamal's door opened, and he stopped for a moment. Crista imagined he was listening to the night, to see if there was any danger. Waiting, Crista and Kayzee barely dared to breathe.

Then Crista heard Jamal's shoes grinding on the pavement. He was walking across the parking lot to the school.

Crista slid the lid up just in time to see Jamal disappear into the building. She opened it all the way, and Kayzee got out.

"Man, that is cramped in there," Kayzee said. "How did you stand it?"

"It wasn't easy."

They both crawled to the back of the truck and jumped out.

"Should we go in?" Kayzee asked.

"If we're going to find out what he's doing, I guess we'd better."

"This gives me the creeps."

They both ran in a slight crouch over to the school. Jamal had blocked the door open by jamming a stick in between the door and the sill.

Crista and Kayzee listened at the door, then they heard voices.

"Who's that?" Kayzee whispered.

"I don't know."

"Is it inside?"

"I don't know. Listen."

They were both quiet, and Crista looked around. Suddenly she gasped. "Look."

There on the highway were two parked cars, only one wasn't a car. One was the gray truck Crista and Kayzee had seen days before following them.

"What are they doing here?" Kayzee asked in alarm.

Crista stared in horror. They had been followed! Both the car and the truck started up and turned into the school lot. Crista's heart began hammering.

"Let's go in," Crista said. "I don't think this is good."

"What will they do?" Kayzee's voice trembled.

"Just go in. We've got to hide. I don't think they're up to good."

·18·
In the School

Closing the door behind them, Crista and Kayzee stepped into the pitch-black hallway. Up ahead they could see a red and white illuminated exit light. Otherwise, all was dark.

"We should have a flashlight," Kayzee said.

"I didn't think of it."

Crista looked at the door. The stick was still stuck in the door jamb. She kicked it out and closed the door. If the people outside were intent on coming after them, this would slow them down. The lock on the door clicked with a comforting sound.

"Please don't let them have keys," Crista said to herself.

"What?" Kayzee asked. She had stepped a few feet down the hall.

"I hope they don't have keys."

"Do you think they'll come after us?"

"I don't know. But let's not wait to find out."

Trembling, Crista guided her feet down the hall. Her rubber soles squeaked on the linoleum. Her heart hammered hard in her chest. The two girls reached the main corridor down to the classrooms. Behind them it went out to the front of the building, the offices, and several classrooms. In front of them was a long line of classrooms that went to a tee, and then spread out in both directions. Crista and Kayzee's classroom was about halfway down on the right.

Suddenly, behind her, she heard the door rattle. Then voices.

"Open up!" A male voice shouted.

"It's them!" Crista said. "What should we do?"

"Don't open up, that's for sure!" Kayzee exclaimed. In the dim light of the exit sign, Crista could see Kayzee's terrified face.

The door rattled again, and Crista heard someone curse. Then she heard a scraping noise and people talking in low tones.

"Let's find Jamal," Kayzee said. "We have to warn him. I have a feeling those people are after him."

The girls hurried down the corridor, their sneakers slapping on the surface with short, punchy whacks. Up ahead, they saw a light. Jamal was in their classroom!

Crista and Kayzee reached the door of the classroom and crouched down, looking in through the long window beside the door. She could see Jamal's flashlight moving around the classroom, then it stopped at Kayzee's desk.

Kayzee and Crista watched.

Then suddenly Kayzee gasped. "I know what he's doing," she whispered.

"What?"

"Remember I showed you the candy bar and note I found in my desk that one day?"

"Yeah."

"Well, there's been one in there every day since. I didn't tell anyone because I was kind of embarrassed about it. But I didn't know who it was. I thought it might be Mrs. Roberts or one of the teachers. But it was Jamal." Her voice took on an awed tone. "He was trying to encourage me."

"Seems like a rather strange way to encourage someone."

"That's Jamal's way. He never likes to be the center of attention. He's always done things like this. When I was little, he would bring things home he found in the street or someplace, and leave them in my room. He would never tell anyone he did it, although we soon figured out it was him. He did the same thing with my mom. One time he gave her a birthday present for every day of the week of her birthday. And all he did was sign it, 'an admirer.' "

"He doesn't sound like the bad person I thought he was."

"It stopped when he started to get in trouble in Atlanta," Kayzee said. "He really changed for a while. But up here, even though he had that problem with firecrackers and stuff, he's been doing really well. That's why I reacted so hard when you told me about following him. I felt kind of...kind of..."

"Protective," Crista put in.

"Yeah. I really care about him. I mean, after all, he is my family."

Crista smiled. "You should care about him."

"Uh oh, here he comes."

The flashlight shone on the doorway and was clearly moving in their direction.

"What should we do?" Crista asked nervously.

"Just tell him we're here!" Kayzee laughed.

The door opened.

"Hi!" Kayzee said gaily, as if nothing were out of the ordinary.

Jamal stared at her. He then shone the light in Crista's eyes.

"What the..."

"Don't say it, Jamal," Kayzee said. "I love you for what you're doing."

"What am I doing?"

"Putting the candy bar in my desk."

Jamal pointed the flashlight at his feet.

"Well, I guess you'd have found out sooner or later."

Kayzee hugged him and gave him a kiss. "I love you for it."

"Yeah, well..." Jamal said. "It wasn't nothin'."

"Yes it was."

Crista listened behind her for sounds of the men. "Kayzee, are you forgetting something?" She tugged on Kayzee's jacket.

Kayzee looked at Crista. "Oh, we've got a slight problem, Jamal."

"What's that?"

"You were followed."

"Followed?"

"By more than us."

"By who?"

"Some men. One of them is driving the truck that followed me and Crista and Jeff a couple times," Kayzee said. "I think it could be trouble."

Jamal gave them a wry look.

"I think we'd better go out another door," Crista said. "But how are we going to get back to the truck? They're in the parking lot."

"Maybe we should go into the office and call the police," Kayzee said.

"Yeah, right, break into the school, break into the office," Jamal said. "They'd only put me away for sixty years."

Kayzee laughed skittishly. "Yeah, that might not be such a great idea."

Suddenly they heard a banging sound that froze them in their tracks. It was the sound of something breaking.

A moment later, voices echoed in the hallway.

"We're in!" someone yelled.

"Find them fast," another voice said.

Crista stared at Jamal and Kayzee. "What are we going to do?" she whispered.

·19·
On the Run

"This way." Jamal led them down the corridor toward the back of the building where the last few classrooms were, as well as the boiler room and the gym.

They raced past the classrooms, their feet slapping on the linoleum.

"Where are we going?" Kayzee cried.

Jamal looked back. Crista turned just in time to see the first flashlights come around the corner. The men were on their trail.

"There they are!" someone shouted.

"What will they do to us?" Kayzee asked fearfully.

Crista grabbed her hand and pulled her along. "Let's not wait to find out."

They reached the corner. Jamal stopped and looked both ways. "What's back here?" he asked There was terror in his voice.

"To the right is the gym," Crista answered, "and next to it the boiler room and then two classrooms. To the left is more classrooms."

"To the right, then," Jamal said. "But wait a second. Get over there." He pointed to the right corridor. Crista and Kayzee hid in the shadows behind the wall.

He shone his flashlight to the left. "This way," he yelled and ran to the left, the flashlight out in front of him. A moment later he turned it off. He stooped low to the ground, hidden by the turn into the left corridor. He then groped across the floor, hurrying to the girls.

"Maybe they'll go to the left," he whispered. "Come on. Try to be quiet. Step easily and put down your feet without making a sound."

The three of them walked up the hall. The men's voices were getting closer but still hadn't made the turn yet.

When Kayzee, Crista, and Jamal reached the gym doors, Jamal turned on the flashlight for just a moment. "In here," he said.

He opened the door silently and stepped inside onto a basketball court. On either side were bleachers, rolled up so they stood against the walls on either side of the court. Above the doors into the gym at either end were two red and white exit lights, shining into the gym, giving it an eerie red glow. But it also illuminated the way. They could see enough of where they were going to get out of sight.

Crista whispered, "I think there's a door behind the bleachers on the far wall. I don't know where it goes."

Jamal turned on his light for just a few seconds. They found their way over to the bleachers. Behind them lay about two feet of room to hide.

"We can wait here," Kayzee said, trembling.

"No," Jamal said, "we have to find a way outta here. We don't want to get trapped. Where's that door, Crista?"

"Up that way," Crista said, pointing.

Jamal squeezed into the space behind the bleachers. Crista and Kayzee followed. No one heard the men outside. Crista hoped they'd gone in the other direction and were completely hoodwinked. So far they'd eluded them. But for how much longer?

They had to get to a phone and call the police, Crista decided. It was no time to worry about whether people would be mad because Jamal had gone into the building at night. That could all be explained.

In the tight space behind the bleachers, it was dark and cool. Their breathing sounded loud and hurried. It felt as if they'd be heard the moment anyone walked into the gym.

Jamal kept walking down toward the door. Crista and Kayzee followed right behind him. In a few moments they came to a split in the bleachers where the door was.

"Where does it go to?" Jamal whispered.

"I don't know," Crista said. "I think the boiler room is next to the gym, but I'm not sure. I've never been in there."

Jamal tried turning the knob. "It's locked," he said.

"I thought it would be," Crista replied. "What do we do now?"

Jamal shone the flashlight on the lock. "I may be able to get into it. But let's go down to the other end. See if there's any other doors out."

They hurried down to the end of the bleachers. There were no more doors behind the bleachers, only doors that went out to another corridor at the end of the gym. Crista saw flashlights gleaming outside those doors. The men were looking for a way in.

"We have to go back," Jamal said, "and open that door."

"But how?" Crista asked.

"I don't know. I have some tricks though." Jamal grinned.

Crista gripped Kayzee's hand.

"Hurry," Kayzee squeaked.

The doors at the end of the gym rattled. "They're locked," a muffled voice said on the outside.

Locked? Crista wondered. Why were the doors at the other end open, where they'd come in? Maybe that was the Lord's doing, Crista thought. Protecting us. She whispered a faint thank you.

"They must be in there," another voice said. "They ain't down the other way. No sign of them. We looked in every classroom."

So Jamal's trick had worked. For the moment.

"Open these doors," a man commanded.

Crista and Kayzee stood with Jamal at the door in the middle of the bleachers. Jamal took out a Swiss army knife from his pocket. He opened the blade. Then he slipped it into the crack between the jamb and the door itself.

"Darn," he said. "It's too tight."

The doors at the end of the gym rattled again. Then they heard something being jammed into the doors.

"They've got a crowbar," Jamal whispered.

"They're going to get in!" Kayzee cried.

Jamal closed the knife and put it back in his pocket. He took out his wallet and fished out a plastic card.

"You have a charge card?" Crista asked.

"It's an old one of my mom's," Jamal replied. "It's out of date. Sometimes it comes in handy."

He slid the card into the door jamb near the lock. "If I can get it in the little beveled part behind the bolt, I can usually beat a lock every time," Jamal said.

"Good grief," Crista commented. "You do know how to get in trouble, don't you."

Jamal only smiled as he shifted the card around. He jiggled the door.

Behind them they heard the men break through the gym doors.

"Find them, quick!" One of the men said.

"Jamal, please," Kayzee whispered, her voice tight.

As Jamal jiggled the door, everyone stopped breathing. The men were making a lot of noise running around the gym, so they couldn't have heard Jamal working on the lock.

"Be quiet." Don't move! One of the men suddenly said.

In the stillness the sound of the jiggling lock seemed to fill the room.

"Over there!" Another man yelled.

Oh, Lord, Crista prayed in her mind, please do something.

Suddenly, Jamal had the door open! They all slid through. Inside the boiler room an eerie green glow touched everything.

"There!" one of the men called as Jamal shut the door behind him.

"They won't be able to get in unless they do the same thing," Jamal said. "Come on. There are plenty of places to hide here."

·20·
The Boiler Room

Two huge boilers sat in the middle of the room, and there were pipes all over the place. The kids stood on a little raised platform. Jamal shone his light.

Behind them, hands banged on the door. Crista jumped.

"We're gonna get you," one of the voices on the other side of the door yelled.

Crista ran down the stairs into the main boiler room. There were all kinds of large drums that looked scary in the dim light. Pipes ran up the side walls into the ceiling and stretched across the top of the ceiling into the rest of the building.

"Air conditioning, heating, everything," Jamal commented.

On the far wall were some stairs going up to another door high above them.

"We've got to find something to block the door," Jamal said.

Crista groped around, peering into drums and onto a worktable against another wall. There were wrenches, screwdrivers, hammers, all kinds of tools, including electrical ones. Jamal picked up a big wrench.

"No, this won't do." He threw the wrench down. "We need a chair or some wooden blocks or something like that to put against the door, to make it more difficult to open. Why doesn't this workbench have a chair?"

Suddenly, the banging on the door stopped, and there was silence. A moment later, Crista heard scratchy noises at the door. The men were trying to do the same thing Jamal had done.

"Hurry," Jamal said. "What can we use?"

Crista looked to the right of one of the boilers. There was a pile of road equipment there, including orange barrels, cones, and some sawhorses.

"The sawhorses!" Crista yelled. "We can lean them up against the door."

"Good idea," Jamal said.

Crista and Kayzee stood on one side and Jamal on the other. The sawhorses were heavy, made of steel. Crista and Kayzee lifted.

"Unnhh, this is heavy," Kayzee said.

"Hurry," Crista huffed.

They dragged the sawhorse across the floor. Crista knew it would be difficult getting it up the stairs, but they had to try. The scratchy noises at the door continued. Any moment the men would get in. Her heart drummed inside her chest like a jackhammer. She did not want to have to face the men on the other side of that door.

The sawhorse screeched and scraped on the concrete floor of the boiler room. The air around them was hot and muggy. Crista felt sweat trickle down her neck. She was breathing hard, trying to get the sawhorse over to the stairs.

"We have to lift now," Jamal said, his voice betraying his fright. "What do those guys want anyway?"

"I don't want to find out," Crista said.

They reached the stairs.

"No, wait a minute." Jamal suddenly stopped. "What right do they have to do this to us? What— are they after me because I'm black? Is that what they want?"

"I don't know," Crista said. "Come on." She looked at Kayzee. Her eyes were wide with fright.

"We have to hurry," Kayzee said low.

Jamal suddenly pushed the sawhorse down and stood there. "These people have no right. Ever since we've been here, we've been harassed and hated, and I've had it."

"Jamal, those men had a bat," Kayzee wailed.

"I don't give a…"

"Don't say it!" Kayzee screamed.

The scratching at the door continued.

"Please hurry," Crista said. "We have to get this up there."

Jamal blinked. "Okay, I'm sorry. Just lost it for a second there." He picked up the sawhorse in one motion and took it up the stairs on his shoulders. Crista and Kayzee stood back, amazed.

He jammed it into place. "There," he yelled at the door. "Get past that."

Suddenly, the door cracked open, banging into the sawhorse. A gap of about four inches opened up. A man's hand groped around for the edge of the sawhorse.

"We gonna nail you, n——," a voice said.

"Yeah, well, I'd like to see you try!" Jamal had drawn out his knife.

"No!" Crista yelled. "Don't, Jamal. It'll just..."

"I'll fight you, man," Jamal yelled, "every last one of you!"

Something crashed against the door, echoing through the room. The sawhorse moved back against the metal railing. The door cracked open another two inches.

"Just come in here!" Jamal was getting hysterical. "I'll fight you!"

"Come on, Kayzee." Crista grabbed her friend. "They've all gone crazy. We have to get out of here and get to a phone. Fast."

"But how?" Kayzee asked.

Crista pointed to the stairway up to the door. "I think that door goes somewhere, maybe to the roof. If we get out on the roof, maybe we can signal someone on the highway. I'm not going to stand here and watch Jamal take on those guys. He's going to get hurt."

Jamal looked down at them. His face and eyes were filled with hatred.

Crista turned. "Come on, Kayzee, we've got to go. If Jamal wants to stay here, let him." She pulled Kayzee by the hand across the boiler room.

There was another bang as the men rammed the door into the sawhorse. The railing shook, but Jamal stood there. He had his knife out, but he didn't look as angry. He just looked scared.

Crista stepped between the two boilers. The heat off them smacked her in the face. The sweat poured down her cheeks. The floor was wet and slick. Noticing a large oil can standing there, Crista realized the floor was a little oily. She tried to be careful, but Kayzee slipped and dragged on her hand. Crista turned around.

"You okay?"

Kayzee got her balance and stood. "It's almost like oil or something."

"Be careful."

Crista looked up at Jamal. There were more bangs as the door bammed into the sawhorse and shook the railing. Jamal stood there, not moving.

Reaching the stairs, Crista started to climb them. They were metal, and the slickness on her soles made her slip a little.

"Don't fall," Kayzee said.

Crista noticed rags hanging on a rack behind the boilers. "Let's wipe off our shoes."

There was another loud bam. The railing jarred

and separated at the joint. It was coming apart.

"Jamal!" Crista yelled. "Please, come."

There was another boom. The sawhorse was knocked back. The door opened wider.

Jamal jumped over the railing and ran toward them. Suddenly, he stopped. "Go," he yelled. "I've got an idea."

He grabbed the oil can, turned around, and sloshed the oil out onto the floor behind him. "This'll slow them down."

There was one more loud bam, then the sawhorse tumbled over the concrete stairs. The door came open all the way, and Crista saw four men in the doorway. One of them had a bat, and a chain hung from a second man's hand.

Crista climbed the stairs. Kayzee was right behind her, and then Jamal. The men pushed into the room and started down the stairs. Jamal watched a second, then yelled at them, "Can't get me, can't get me!"

Crista couldn't believe he was doing that, but she couldn't help but chuckle as the first man hit the floor, slid on the oil, and fell flat on his back.

"Watch out!" he yelled. "Oil all over the place."

Reaching the door, Crista looked it over. There was no door handle, just a little hinge sticking out at an angle and above it a dead bolt that opened from their side. She turned it.

"Get them!" one of the men yelled. She looked back and saw the men slipping all over the floor.

One was trying to walk very carefully across the concrete, but another of the men grabbed him and they both went down. It was almost comical. For the first time, she saw that the men all had their faces covered. One wore a bandanna over his nose and mouth like some bad cowboy. The others were all wearing ski masks. It gave Crista the creeps.

The door opened as Crista pushed on it. She glanced encouragingly at Kayzee, whose eyes were still wide and darting about. Jamal came up behind them.

The cool air of the night slammed into Crista's face, and she suddenly felt better. The sweat on her skin suddenly felt cool. She stepped onto the roof. The stars above them looked the same—bright, spread out, distant, fearless. Did they know what was going on down on this little pocket of planet earth?

The roof was covered with small white angular stones, the kind that looked marbled. The kids all looked out over the roof of the school. It seemed to stretch on for miles.

"Where to?" Jamal asked, almost casual. "They'll be up here in a minute. We can't block this door."

"Let's run for...wait!" Crista said. "There's a ladder, down to the ground somewhere. Do you remember, Kayzee?"

Shaking her head with fear, Kayzee looked back at the door.

"It's by the kitchen," Crista suddenly remembered. "Which way is the kitchen?"

Kayzee turned around. "That way," she said, pointing to the main section of the school.

They all began running. Stones kicked up under their feet. They were a third of the way across, when the door blasted open.

"There they are!" the man with the bat yelled.

·21·
Through the Woods

"I hope you're right about this," Crista cried as Kayzee, Jamal, and she ran for the corner where the ladder was supposed to be. The metal ladder offered a way to get on the roof that kids sometimes used when playing around the school, although it was illegal and carried stiff penalties for those who violated the rules.

In less than thirty seconds they reached the corner. Crista looked over. There was no ladder.

"It's not here!" she cried.

She turned. The men hurried across the rooftop toward them. They'd catch up in seconds.

"The other corner!" Kayzee yelled.

The three of them jumped up and sprinted toward the next corner. The men veered off to the left, trying to cut them off. Even if they reached the ladder, Crista knew, they might not have enough time to get down.

They reached the corner. The ladder was there.

Crista breathed with some relief, but her heart continued its pounding. "Over, over!" she cried to Kayzee.

Kayzee didn't hesitate. She backed over the edge and started down. The men yelled and screamed at them, but Kayzee didn't stop. Then Crista started down.

"Go! Go!" Jamal said. "Go!"

Crista stepped as quickly as she could, but Jamal couldn't wait. The men were almost there.

As Crista kept on going down the ladder, Jamal hung off the side of the roof. He stretched out all the way, then dropped the one story to the ground. His knees came up into his chest and knocked the wind out of him, but he was on the ground. Crista touched down right next to him.

"You okay?"

"Let's go!" Jamal wheezed, grabbing Kayzee's hand.

"Into the woods," Crista cried. The truck was on the other side of the building, and Crista knew instinctively they'd never make it there. The men were already clambering over the edge, yelling and shouting at the kids.

"We're gonna nail you," one of the men with the ski masks yelled.

Crista shivered. Why did people hate others so much?

Jamal and Kayzee were out ahead of her, but she caught up easily.

"We can hide in the woods," Jamal said.

"It's only a little strip," Crista replied. "On the other side is the dam. Maybe we can cross the dam."

"They'll still be able to follow us," Jamal called behind him.

Crista turned to see what was happening. One of the men was on the ground now, but he waited for the others. That gave Crista hope. They already had fifty yards between them and the men, and they were adding distance with each second. Maybe there was some place to hide in the woods.

And then again, maybe not. Crista's heart sank. It was just a short stretch over to the rocky slope of the dam. The starry moonlit sky contrasted the events going on on the ground.

The kids raced past the kindergarten playground equipment and reached the woods. The group of men was not far behind. Sticks broke under Crista's feet. She gripped Kayzee's hand, and the two girls got in front of Jamal.

"What do they want?" Crista huffed as she looked ahead. The woods were thinning out and the path was rockier. Large stones and rocks ready to trip them poked up through the soil and lay on top.

"They want to hurt us," Kayzee answered, breathing heavy herself.

"But why?" Crista asked.

"Because we're black."

"But what's that have to do with it?" Crista said as they made their way over the stones. The monstrous dam loomed above them. The near side, where the kids were, was a jumble of giant rocks and boulders all laid up against the back of the dam.

The spillway cut the middle of the dam, allowing water over the edge. Right now it was dry. The lake wasn't that high.

On the top of the dam sat a layer of asphalt that allowed trucks to drive across, although they had to be small. The three kids reached the cyclone fence that made the boundary between the edge of the woods and the dam.

"This way," Crista said, climbing over a large rock in her path. The beaten dirt path led towards the dam. Crista knew of a hole in the fence that kids used when playing around the dam. She hoped it hadn't been repaired.

She could hear the men stumbling around in the trees. Crista knew the path in this area and that had helped their escape. Crista came up here frequently, with her dad.

Jamal said, "Where are we going?"

"There's a break in the fence up a ways. We can get out onto the dam and cross it," Crista answered. She felt hot, almost feverish. Kayzee coughed several times.

"They might not know of the break," Crista added. "If they don't, it'll delay them."

"Well, where is it?" The anger in Jamal's voice was unmistakable.

"I'm looking, I'm looking," Crista replied.

She held Kayzee's hand tightly. Jamal kept turning back and looking toward the trail where they'd come out of the woods. The men still hadn't appeared.

Crista breathed hard as she clambered over the stones. It would be too easy to slip and twist an ankle, so she tried to be careful. She said to Kayzee, "Plant your foot solidly. Watch out for slippery areas where moss is growing."

Someone appeared below them. Crista couldn't see him clearly, but she saw the bat. He yelled, "Up there!"

Crista looked ahead. She saw the flap of Cyclone fence where the gap was.

Suddenly two more men stepped out on the path in front of them. They had gone through the woods and come out on the trail above the kids. At that moment all hope of surprise and escape was dashed.

"Hurry!" Crista yelled to Kayzee and Jamal. If they weren't fast, they'd be cut off.

"I'm going. I'm going," Kayzee seethed back.

The two men above them sighted the kids. "There they are! Close in!"

Below them two other men moved quickly over the stones.

Crista reached the gap. "Someone closed it!" she gasped.

·22·

Danger at the Dam

Jamal leaned down and pulled up on the fence. It wasn't anchored. A small opening appeared. He jerked it up higher. The men were getting closer. Jamal's breath was labored and piercing.

"Slide through," he gasped.

Kayzee got down on her hands and knees. She went through headfirst, just barely fitting under. Crista followed.

"Jamal!" Crista said as the men came after him.

He darted back into the woods. "Go on!" he yelled. "I'll catch up."

"Get the boy," the man with the bat yelled when he saw Jamal running. "We'll get the others."

Two men went after Jamal. Crista and Kayzee made their way up to the dam. Moments later, they stood on top.

"Where's Jamal?" Kayzee wailed.

"He's coming. He's got to come," Crista cried, unsure of anything she said. She prayed out loud, "Please, Lord, help Jamal."

The men were pushing hard on the fence, pulling

up on it to make a gap. One of them said, "Let's climb over."

He started up the fence, sticking the toe of his boot into the little square holes in the wire fence. He slipped and slid down, causing the bandanna he was wearing to slip off his face.

Crista recognized him. It was Danny Kluziewski's father! She'd seen him at school a few times with Danny. He had a dark face and deep set eyes that looked black and sinister. He was unshaved, with a stubble of gray hair on his chin. He looked angry and determined.

"Across the dam," Crista said.

"But what about Jamal?" Kayzee asked.

"He can take care of himself," Crista replied, not knowing what else to say. She hoped it was true.

A moment later, she spotted Jamal. He had come out of the woods a way up from the dam on the shoreline. The fence ran along the shore and right into the water. He hit the fence and started climbing. The two men were right behind him, but Jamal was over before they reached him.

"Keep going!" Jamal yelled to the girls.

Crista shifted her attention to the other two men. One of them was trying to slide under the fence, but so far he'd had no luck. The other man was holding it up.

The two men after Jamal tried climbing the fence where Jamal had gone over, but they were both too heavy to make it. Jamal quickly wove his way over the rocks. "Go! Go!" he yelled again. He soon stepped onto the lower end of the dam. Crista and Kayzee sped across the top of the dam, sending stray stones spinning over the edge. Crista refused to look to her right where the dam sloped down to the huge rocks in the valley below. She didn't like heights and this dam was high up. She gripped Kayzee's hand tightly.

Leaping past the last little cleft in the dam, Jamal stepped onto the top. Crista and Kayzee tiptoed across the iron grate that spanned the gap in the dam where the water was let out over the spillway. Their sneakers rattled on the metal. The men still hadn't gotten through the fence, but the two who had followed Jamal had now joined the two others. With three of them pulling up on the fence, they'd surely make enough of an opening for them to get through, Crista knew. There wasn't much time.

Crista and Kayzee reached the other side of the dam. Jamal's feet thudded on the steel grate over the dam spillway. Crista looked ahead and saw the fence on the far side. What to do now?

A moment later, Kayzee pointed, "A boat. Look, a boat."

It was tied up to a tree along the edge of the woods on the far side of the dam. Oars crossed in the back of the boat, metal ringed oarlocks holding them in place.

"They couldn't get to us out in the water," Kayzee said.

Crista nodded. "Good idea. Come on."

They ran down from the dam onto the pile of rocks that lined the edges of the dam. The boat knocked gently against the rocks. It was tied securely, but there was no lock or chain. It probably belonged to a local fisherman, Crista figured, who wouldn't mind them borrowing it in an emergency.

Crista and Kayzee clambered across the rocks, balancing themselves with their hands and crawling along in a crouch.

The four men had gotten through the fence and were now running across the dam toward Jamal.

Reaching the rocks, Jamal climbed down toward the girls. Soon they all stood next to the boat. The men stood on the top of the dam, looking at them. The one Crista was sure was Danny Kluziewski's father called to them.

"You're caught, kids. Give up."

Jamal said to Crista and Kayzee, "Get into the boat."

The man said again, "We have no gripe with you. You can go."

Crista suddenly realized the man was talking to her. She looked at Kayzee and Jamal, who both hung their heads.

"You can go, little girl. We'll let you pass."

Crista looked up at the men. "And then you'll hurt my friends."

"They're not the kind of people we want in this town."

"Who's 'we'?" Crista asked defiantly.

"Us. People like us. Responsible citizens."

Crista's heart swelled with anger. "And what will you do to my friends if I leave?"

"We will deal with them. That's none of your business."

"Why don't you take off your masks?"

"We're giving you one last chance," the man said, ignoring her question. "Either go now, or suffer the consequences."

One of the men spoke into a walkie-talkie, but Crista couldn't hear what he was saying.

"Why are you hiding behind masks?" Crista asked again. "What are you afraid of?"

The man spoke calmly. "We are not hiding. Do you want to go or not?" The man with the bat slowly lifted the bat and punched it into his hand.

Crista started to get into the boat. "I'm not leaving my friends."

The man with the bat started down toward them. The one with the walkie-talkie spoke frantically into it, then he nodded to the others.

"You can't escape," the man with the bat yelled.

Jamal pushed the boat off the rocks. Crista sat at the oars and got ready to row. She knew she could row about a mile across the lake to her cabin and get her father. It would take some time, but it was a way to escape. Surely the men wouldn't follow them into the water. There were no other boats nearby.

Or were there?

In the distance, Crista heard the whirring of a boat motor. She tried to force away the fear that clutched at her throat, but now she was scared more than ever. Out on the lake they were sitting ducks. If these men had a boat in hiding somewhere, with others in it, they were caught.

The man with the walkie-talkie called, "In a moment, our boat will be here. You can't escape. We'll still let you go, little girl. So give up. These people aren't your friends."

Crista glanced at Kayzee and suddenly hugged her tightly. "Kayzee is my friend!"

She whirled around. "And so is Jamal. If you hurt them, you hurt me. We're friends, and I'm not leaving them!"

The man laughed. "Fool!"

·23·

Nowhere to Run

The sound of the boat roared closer. Someone was coming from the cove, Crista thought. There was no way out this time.

She rowed out in front of the dam. The water was deep there, she knew. The roar of the engine on the mysterious boat became clearer. Crista swallowed hard. Should they try for the other shore? Should they get back to the woods, back to the truck?

Two lights appeared through the trees—red and green. And a white one further back. A boat. It was not coming to rescue them.

The men on shore cheered.

Crista began to row frantically. Jamal sat in the front looking dejectedly at the boat coming toward them. Kayzee sat frozen in the back. She looked down at her feet.

Crista sensed that everyone was giving up.

"No!" she screamed. "They won't get us!"

Now the boat came into full view. A searchlight on the front of the boat scanned the area, then came to rest on the little fishing boat. Crista blinked from the stark light and rowed furiously toward shore. But it was over fifty yards to the trees where they could get off. They couldn't go back. They couldn't go forward. They were stuck.

The motorboat slowed down, and Crista felt despair lodge in her throat. It was really over.

The two men in the boat wore masks, too. The men on shore waved and cheered. The boat was coming alongside.

Crista said to Jamal, "Take an oar, we can fight them off."

"It's over," Jamal muttered darkly. "It's over."

"No!" Crista yelled. "Take an oar."

She lifted one of the oars out of the oarlock and held it up like a jousting lance. The motorboat came straight toward them.

Suddenly, Crista whipped around. "I know who you are!" she called. "You're Danny Kluziewski's father! I know who you are and I'll tell the police."

The men just laughed.

The motor rumbled low, nearly idling now. As Crista held up the oar, one of the men grabbed it and jerked it out of her hand, almost pulling her overboard. Jamal sat in the front of the boat watching, doing nothing. Kayzee, though, got up and grabbed the second oar. She whipped it over her head, but the driver tore it away from her hands. As he did so, Kayzee lost her balance. She cried out, "Help!"

A second later, she fell backwards into the lake.

Crista screamed.

Jamal was on his feet now.

Crista crouched down and looked over the side. Kayzee broke the surface but immediately sank again.

"She can't swim," Jamal cried. "She can't swim. I can't either!"

Crista tore off her jacket. The men on shore were laughing. The two men in the motorboat laughed, too. Jamal stood now, looking into the dark water. He said low and frightened, "You've gotta get her, Crista." There was raw terror in his voice.

Crista pulled off her sneakers. Then, looking hard into the water, she dove in.

The chill surged through her. The water felt black and confusing. She could see the lights above her, but she couldn't see anything going down. Where was Kayzee? She had to find her, and quick.

Crista prayed frantically in her mind as she searched the water for a sign of Kayzee. It was all so dark, she could do little more than flail around in the water, trying to find something to touch. She knew the water was deep there at the dam, and if Kayzee was sinking, there was little hope of finding her. The water was so cold, she felt frozen through to her very bones.

Where was Kayzee?

Please, Lord, Crista prayed in her mind. Please let me find her.

She broke the surface. "Jamal! Where is she?"

Jamal stood in the boat peering over the edge, paddling slightly, looking this way and that. "I don't see her!"

Crista treaded water in a circle. "She can't be too deep."

Ten feet away there was a sputtering. Something came to the surface. "Help!" It was Kayzee.

As Kayzee sank again, Crista swam with all her might toward the place where Kayzee had gone down. When she reached the little circle of rippling water, she dove.

Again, the darkness was so great she could see little more than a few inches in front of her. Crista knew Kayzee was right there! Where was she now?

Crista moved in the water, trying to feel every which way, hoping to hit anything. Then she felt her foot strike something. She swiveled around, reached, touched something.

Hair!

She grabbed and pulled. It was Kayzee.

Crista dragged Kayzee to the surface. When they got there, Kayzee was still in the moonlight, not breathing. Crista sputtered for Jamal to hold out a hand. If only they had the oars!

Crista set her arm across Kayzee's chest as she'd learned in lifesaving class the summer before. She swam sidestroke toward the boat.

Suddenly, she heard shouting on the shore. She couldn't make it out, but Jamal was pointing, and the motorboat roared off. What was going on?

Water splashed into Crista's eyes and her body felt heavy. She reached up and Jamal's strong hand grabbed hers.

"Pull in Kayzee and give her mouth-to-mouth," Crista cried, garbling her words as waves from the motorboat splashed into her face. She hung onto the side of the rowboat, pushing on Kayzee's arms as Jamal dragged her inside.

"The police," Jamal said. "The police are here."

Crista turned to look at the shore, but waves splashed into her face. She couldn't see anyone.

"Those men are running," Jamal said. "The police are after them." Jamal put his mouth against Kayzee's, and immediately began CPR.

The water hugged her body and Crista felt so cold, her teeth chattered repeatedly and her legs jerked in the water. She pulled herself up on the transom of the boat. Jamal continued to blow air into Kayzee's throat, and suddenly she coughed, spit up water, and breathed.

"Thank God," Crista sighed as she rolled into the boat.

On the shore she heard voices, some shouting, and a bullhorn. And then one voice in particular: "Jamal, Kayzee, are you okay?"

It was Mrs. Jackson.

Crista blinked and looked toward shore. Through the bleariness she spotted Jeff and Mrs. Jackson standing on the rocks.

"Crista, are you all right?" Mrs. Jackson called.

"Yeah, just frozen," Crista responded with chattering teeth. She tried to clear her mind. "What's going on?" she murmured to Jamal.

Mrs. Jackson called, "Jeff came to tell me what happened. When you didn't come back, he decided we'd better come down and look for you. We called the police from my car phone. They're in the woods now, searching for the men."

Jeff waved.

"They threw the oars overboard," Jamal said to Crista. "There they are. Paddle over with me."

Crista hugged her body but finally reached out with one hand and helped Jamal paddle over to the two oars floating in the water. Kayzee lay on the backseat, breathing and shivering. Crista put her dry jacket around Kayzee's shoulders.

"No, you put it on," Kayzee said through chattering teeth. "You're as cold as I am."

"No." Crista helped Kayzee put on the jacket.

Jamal began rowing toward shore. In a minute, the boat knocked up against the rocks. Crista helped Kayzee out.

"You nearly drowned!" Mrs. Jackson said, crying.

"I'm okay," Kayzee said. "Crista dove in and pulled me up."

"Crista, how can I ever thank you?"

"Get us to some warmth," Crista said, hardly able to get the words out. Jeff led them across the dam to the fence. The police had cut a large hole in it, and they were able to pass through without hindrance.

They found their way back to the cars, and soon Crista sat in Mrs. Jackson's car, letting the air from the heater blow over her face.

"My baby," Mrs. Jackson said, weeping and crying as she held Kayzee. "They wanted to hurt my baby!"

Crista's eyes teared as the warm air nuzzled her face. Jamal and Jeff were talking behind her, but she couldn't make out what they were saying. She felt sleepy, almost dreamy.

And then suddenly her father was there and people all over the place. She sat in her dad's Cherokee for the ride home, letting even hotter air waft over her.

Finally, she slid into the fresh sheets of her own bed, in her own pajamas. Her father whispered, "You really did something tonight, honey. You outdid yourself. I'm proud of you."

Crista just murmured, "Good night, Daddy."

"Good night, honey. I love you."

"I love you, too."

Then everything was black until morning.

·24·
Friends to the End

"Apparently, they had this secret society—to keep Jews, Blacks, and Hispanics out of the area," Dr. Mayfield said to Mrs. Jackson, Crista, and the others as they gathered around the dining room table, partaking of roast chicken, peas, buttered corn, and mashed potatoes. Mrs. Jackson and Kayzee had come over and helped Crista prepare the meal. Over the last three days, the police had finally caught the group of men who had harassed new residents for years.

"They beat up one man a couple of years ago," Jamal added. "I read that yesterday. They wore masks, and the man is now testifying. They found a bunch of weapons in one of the houses, too."

"When you get into it," Jeff said, "you really get into it, Crista."

"It's not my fault," Crista answered, blowing her nose. Ever since their escapade in the water, both Kayzee and Crista had gotten bad colds. Dr. Mayfield was treating them with bed rest, chicken broth, and the vow that they not take anything else into their own hands—at least for the next week.

"So they're very lucky to have escaped the way they did," Mrs. Jackson said, looking fondly at Kayzee, Jamal, and Crista. "You could really have been hurt."

"They found cans of the spray paint, too," Jeff put in. "In the truck. So it was them all along."

"And not Jamal," Kayzee said. Everyone laughed. It was quite a joke now that Crista had thought Jamal could possibly have written some of those words just so he could go back to Atlanta.

Crista shrugged, "You win some, you lose some."

"Anyway, next time you think you've made the great criminal capture of the century," Dr. Mayfield said, "consult some parents first. Okay?"

"Okay!" Crista coughed and sneezed. "Can we talk about something else?"

"Sure," Mrs. Jackson said. "How about the fact that I have entered your portrait of our family in a little contest, Crista."

Turning to Mrs. Jackson, Crista looked surprised. "You have?"

"It's just a little thing," Mrs. Jackson replied. "But it could win you some money. I know we could all use that."

Crista was too amazed to answer. Then she stammered, "That's great. When do I get to spend it, Dad?"

"First you have to win it," Dr. Mayfield said with a wink.

Crista shook her head. "There's always a catch."

Everyone laughed except Jamal, who said, "Just one thing, Crista, I've been wondering about. When those men offered you a chance to go, why didn't you take it?"

Crista thought about it. "Friends don't desert friends. No matter what."

"So we're friends then?" Jamal asked.

"Me and Kayzee anyway," Crista said with a grin.

Jamal laughed. "Oh, and I suppose you'll be tracking me every time I take a ride in that truck from now on."

"That's right." Crista nodded. "Right in the toolbox. They'll call me the tool woman."

Everyone laughed again and began to eat. It was a good meal. But for Crista it was especially wonderful. She was with her friends, and she knew no one could take them away.

About the Author

Mark Littleton is the author of over 24 books, including the recent *Fillin' Up* in the Up Series of teen devotionals. He lives with his two children, Nicole and Alisha, in Columbia, Maryland.

The Action Never Stops in
The Crista Chronicles
by Mark Littleton

Secrets of Moonlight Mountain

When an unexpected blizzard traps Crista on Moonlight Mountain with a young couple in need of a doctor, Crista must brave the storm and the dark to get her physician father. Will she make it in time?

Winter Thunder

The odd circumstances surrounding Mrs. Oldham's broken windows all point to Crista's friend Jeff as the culprit in the recent cabin break-ins. What is Jeff trying to hide? Will Crista be able to prove his innocence?

Robbers on Rock Road

When the clues fall into place regarding the true identity of the cabin-wreckers, Crista and her friends find themselves facing terrible danger! Can they stop the robbers on Rock Road before someone gets hurt?

Escape of the Grizzly

A grizzly is on the loose on Moonlight Mountain! Who will find the bear first—the sheriff's posse or the circus workers? Crista knows there isn't much time—the bear has to be found quickly. But where, and how?

Danger on Midnight Trail

Crista can't stand her cousin Sarah, who does *everything* better. When an overnight hike into the mountains turns into a nightmare, can Crista and Sarah put aside their differences to save Crista's dad?

Capturing the Spirit
of the Next Generation. . .
The Class of 2000
by Ginny Williams

Second Chances

At 15 years old, Kelly finds her life in sudden turmoil when her widowed father decides to remarry. Struggling with bitter feelings, Kelly determines that she'll never accept her father's wife.

A Matter of Trust

God changed Kelly's heart, but now she's finding it difficult sometimes for her actions to follow. Conflict at home threatens to tear the family apart.

Lost-and-Found Friend

Kelly's friend Brent is a very sensitive, very intense person who is adept at hiding his troubles. When pressures at home become overwhelming, Brent makes a desperate decision.

A Change of Heart

Julie had always thought her faith was strong. But when she makes the school's tennis team and meets new friends who are into the party scene, she finds herself questioning what she believes.

Spring Fever

Kelly and Greg have a great relationship. Why, then, is she interested in the new guy at school who wants to got out with her? Kelly tries to enjoy both relationships—but with disastrous results.

Find Adventure and Excitement in
The Maggie's World Series
by Eric Wiggin

Maggie: Life at The Elms

Maggie's father died at the Battle of Gettysburg, and the man her mother is going to marry has a son who Maggie just can't stand! She asks for permission to live with her grandpa in the deep woods of northern Maine—at his special home, The Elms.

Little does Maggie know how much her life is about to change—all because of a sharp-tongued girl at a logging camp, and surprising lessons about friendship and forgiveness.

Maggie's Homecoming

After two years in the deep woods with Grandpa, Maggie is eager to return home. She and her stepbrother, Jack, must learn to get along—and to everyone's amazement, they do!

One Saturday she and Jack decide to explore a long-abandoned farmhouse around the mountainside—only to find out the place isn't abandoned after all. . . .

Maggie's Secret Longing

At sixteen, Maggie is now the new schoolmarm in charge of the education of Laketon Junction's children—a mischievous, fun-loving bunch of young rascals. Every day is filled with challenges and surprises!

But becoming an adult is not always easy, Maggie discovers. Torn between her bright, eager students and the young, exciting Terry MacAlester, Maggie's heart faces a difficult choice.